Editing by The Crimson Wordsmith
Cover Design by Dawn Burdett
Internal Formatting by Dean Shawker

MYSTWOOD

VICTOR NANDI

For everyone who once loved beyond reason—and lost beyond repair.

CONTENTS

PROLOGUE

Basil's warm hands grazed over Ophelia's skin as she lay on the grass beside him.

The moonlit forest stood around them, stars winking through the drifting sheets of cloud as the two made love. An owl hooted across the glade and perched up on a tree, watching.

They surrendered to their physical yearnings like wild animals—conscious of nothing around them—not even the sky beginning to light up in a gentle viridian glow. The wind eased and the chirping of crickets faded away, leaving only Ophelia's soft moans in the eerie stillness.

The glow dispersed into strands, swirling over the clouds before converging into a dazzling disk of emerald.

Ophelia flinched when she became aware of the sky. With a violent push, she thrust Basil away, just as an unending bolt of viridescence struck her. She screeched in agony while Basil could only watch in fear as the blinding streak of light rained its wrath upon Ophelia's delicate little body.

***

The outline of the man shuffled through the woods, huge, lizard-like creatures on his tail.

He hobbled down a ridge, panting and stumbling to the ground, before pulling himself up using the bushes for leverage, then running again, determined not to give up. Inside, his wounds screamed a symphony, with crimson lines streaming from the gory hollows of his eye sockets. But, teeth gritted, he did not let out the shriek he'd forced down.

Sightless, he fumbled into the valley through the thorny undergrowth, his body smudging patches of fresh blood on trees he bumped into.

A tree root at the edge of a trench caught his foot and he tripped, crashing down onto the rocks at the bottom. A stifled cry spilled out of his mouth as his legs crunched under him.

A growling raged nearer.

Spikes of pain were shooting through his body. It seemed like this was the end, but he refused to yield. He knew it was no longer possible to outrun the creatures—his only option was to hide. He kept clawing at the ground, desperate to climb back up the ridge.

He heard the jagged fluttering of wings and could feel the creatures herding on the trench's edge above him. His hands fumbled on the walls, frantically searching for a refuge.

But then, he heard the growling dive at him.

SEVERAL DECADES LATER

CHAPTER 1

Clad in red, three mounted soldiers cantered through the woods, the glow of their lanterns smothered under thick fog.

The first light of day was still a good two hours away, but they couldn't wait until sunrise. It was a pressing matter.

The woods sprawled over several hundred acres of hills. Pine, fir, aspen, and dogwood rose from mossy undergrowth which had lain relatively untouched since the dawn of time. The place smelled of ancientness, the only sign of civilization being a dirt road snaking through the wilderness.

The riders moved down the path, their leader's searching eyes peering into the dark.

"Why on earth would he take this path?" Lance grumbled at the back in a low voice, his long mane flowing around a face which looked to have lived through a fair few street fights.

"Well, they all take this path for the same reason," Timothy, a stocky man in his forties with the voice of a wimp and the face of an otter, replied. "It's faster."

"It was a rhetorical question, Tim," Lance sneered. "I would be in bed with Gracie if he *hadn't*."

"Thought her name was Bessie."

"Could be." Lance shrugged. "Can't keep track of all the names."

"How do you manage to crawl in with so many women without—"

"Well," Lance cut Tim short. "Women find me irresistible."

"I was going to say 'without your wife knowing.' Anyway, if you think you're so irresistible"—Tim snorted—"why doesn't your charm work on Claire?"

"My charm works on women, Tim."

"What do you mean?" Tim raised his eyebrows "She is very much a—"

"I don't care about her body," Lance interrupted. "On the inside, she's more of a man than you'll ever be."

Tim stared at him. "Thought a woman's body was all you care about."

"Hey!"

Lance and Tim's heads shot up to look at their leader who was trotting ahead of them.

"Look." Claire held up her lantern, her vigilant, blue eyes filled with apprehension.

The three cantered to the wooden carriage sitting stranded on the path twenty yards further on. Pulling up, they stepped down from their horses.

Tim frowned. "Abandoned?"

Claire shone her lantern inside the empty carriage.

"Thieves?" Lance clenched his rifle.

Claire shook her head. "No sign of struggle."

"Wild animals?" Tim said.

"No blood," replied Claire.

"Where did they disappear to then?" Tim asked.

Claire observed the ground under the light and didn't answer.

Tim placed his lantern on the grass and cupped his hands around his mouth. "Anyone there?"

The woods gaped back at him.

"They stopped the carriage willingly," Claire said, following the tire marks. "Got down and walked into the woods"—she studied the footprints and pointed at a trampled fern at the side of the path—"that way."

"Why would they do that?" Tim asked incredulously.

Claire pulled the rifle from her back. "Let's find out." She entered the woods, following the trail of trodden bushes.

Tim and Lance joined her.

"Mister Canterbury?" Claire called out.

"It's *chancellor*," Tim corrected her.

"You can call him that when we find him," Lance murmured. "That is *if* we find him…"

Tim ignored the remark. "Chancellor Canterbury, *sir*?"

Lance scoffed at Tim's idiocy. "Save it, Tim."

The three silhouettes kept moving through the fog.

Claire stopped abruptly.

"What is it?"

"The trail…"

"What about it?" Tim leaned over her shoulder.

"It's gone."

"Just like that?" Lance exclaimed.

Claire nodded.

Lance pulled out a machete.

"What are you doing?" Claire asked.

Lance slashed at branches and stomped through. "Looking."

Claire and Tim watched him vanish behind a curtain of fog.

"So, what do we do?"

"Let him take the east," Claire said. "I'll head up north. You go west. She paused. "We've got to find the chancellor, Tim, by any means necessary."

"Yes," Tim's voice grew somber. "He was our guest. Maybe one of the most esteemed guests to visit Winsden in a long time. It would be a shame if we fail to find out what happened to him quickly."

"He is our guest, Tim." Claire put her hand on his shoulder. "He *is*."

Tim gave an understanding nod, and the two went separate ways.

***

Claire moved through the bushes. Fog had already swallowed the glow of Lance's lamp, and when she looked to the other side, she saw Tim's light had faded too. Claire glanced up at the trees towering above her. Draped in white screens of mist, they all looked identical.

It was difficult to keep track of directions, but Claire plodded through the undergrowth, knowing the trail of flattened lichens under her boots would guide her back.

She reached a clearing and looked around reflexively. There was no sign of the chancellor, but as her gaze swept over the ground behind her, a strange thing caught her attention. Moving the lantern closer, Claire stared at a bush, her forehead creased. Its leaves, which she had stomped upon just a second ago, were decompressing back into shape, as if by some invisible force. Surprised, she peered at the path she had taken. There was no sign of her footfalls.

The place was lit up by a weird glow, and Claire looked up. A soft, luminous tinge of chartreuse flickered through the fog in the distant sky.

She stood, staring, her brows knitted together.

The light hovered for a moment and then streaked away, farther into the eastern part of the forest. Clasping her rifle, Claire ran after it to investigate.

CHAPTER 2

That sound...that deafening sound—is it in my head?

Gertrude woke up with a start.

What if it isn't in my head?

The old woman crawled out of the rug of parched straws she had gathered for the winter.

BANG!

Her delicate frame quivered like a leaf as something bashed against her window for a second time.

Hunched, Gertrude limped across the damp floor of her haggardly shack to the door. She could hear a clamor outside—people moving around frantically, talking, screaming. It was difficult to figure out what they were saying, but she could tell they were agitated.

Holding onto the door with trembling hands, Gertrude shivered, unable to muster the courage to open it, as thoughts flittered through her mind.

When the yelling finally moved away, the old woman parted the door slightly and peeked. A couple of lumpy shapes lay huddled together on the ground under her window.

Raising the flame, Gertrude crept out with the lantern. The shapes were two adult cats, black as night, cut open from belly to mouth, their entrails scattered over the grass. The window upon which they had been hurled was smeared with their blood.

Gertrude peered at the wall. It was scrawled with the word DIE.

Just another day. Heaving a deep sigh of relief, she went inside and fetched a piece of cloth to wipe away the bloody scribbles.

CHAPTER 3

Lance strode up the hill, hacking through the branches on his way. The ground was soft there, the air tasting thicker as he moved onward.

He took a step and stumbled, the machete slipping from his grip, and the lantern rolling across the grass, illuminating the object he'd tripped over.

It was a body. A human body. A few feet away, under a tree, lay another one. Faces ripped off. Chests torn up. Skulls crushed, as if by enormous weights.

Lance pulled away in horror.

A chilly breeze whistled through the trees.

Picking up the lantern, he held it up over the corpses.

Stripped clean of flesh, the mangled bones of their arms and legs glistened under the lantern's light. The torsos had been shredded into gooey mulches of tattered organs—slashes of teeth and razor-sharp claws covering them.

Lance forced his eyes to their faces. The disfigured remains of gnawed tissues and exploded eyeballs stared back at him.

Beneath the brain-spattered jaw of one of the skulls, a circular, metallic object lay half-buried in the white sludge.

Lance brought the light closer.

It was a gold-plated pocket watch. The engraved initials 'R.C.' glittered on its back.

Lance's mouth moved to mutter two words. "Raymond Canterbury."

Just then, sprays of green light filled the place. Lance glanced up. An emerald dash had lit up the sky overhead.

"What the fuck?" Lance grimaced as bright silhouettes of two women emerged from the clouds.

With wings on their backs flapping, they drifted down like a pair of angels, a thin layer of halo framing their ethereal bodies.

Descending before Lance, they looked at the ground. Horror tainted their faces as they eyed the corpses.

Lance kept staring at them, too stunned to move.

They turned to Lance. Those eyes exuded a heavenly shine, but he could read the distress in them. It seemed to Lance they wanted to comfort him but had no words to do so.

Slowly, their wings shrank back, and the intensity of their halos reduced, as if to ease Lance's eyes. The sheet of soft radiance clothing them hardly concealed anything of their glorious bodies, and Lance bet his life he would not find such beauty anywhere.

One of them finally spoke. "Do not be troubled by what you cannot change."

The anguish in her mellifluous voice pained Lance. He kept gazing at her. So overwhelming was their presence, the grisly images of the chancellor and the coachman melted from his mind.

"You shall be protected," the other angel assured. "Is there anyone else with you?"

Lance couldn't speak, he could only move his head from side to side.

CHAPTER 4

Claire's muddled thoughts churned over everything she had witnessed in the woods, the latest being the spectacle in the sky far away—fairy-like beings drifting out of it. Claire had heard of angels and fairies in stories, but never had she believed they truly existed—let alone seeing one with her own two eyes.

She kept watching the sky in the distance. After the angelic beings had emerged, the glow seemed to have converged upon the hill to the east, lighting up the trees over there in an unusual, virescent hue.

Claire didn't know what to make of it—in fact, she didn't know what to make of any of the absurdities she had encountered.

She shuffled on, her mind preoccupied.

How did the bushes restore back in shape so fast? What is the green light? Questions kept pestering her. Things just did not make sense. *Am I dead? Is this the spirit world?* Bizarre thoughts kept piling in. *What if the light is leading me into the afterlife? What if those angels that came down—*

Claire stopped. The light was disappearing. It wasn't moving away; the gleam was just fading out. Tossing the gun around her shoulder, Claire rushed ahead, desperate to catch hold of it before it vanished.

The light shrank into a chartreuse globe the size of a fist. Then a cold wind swept down the hill, carrying a growl that pressed into her ears—muffled, yet bone-chilling, almost unearthly.

Claire paused and peered into the fog, but the glow was gone, as if the angelic flame had been snuffed out by a sudden, demonic gust of wind. Holding the weapon in her hand, she moved forward.

The subdued growling was getting louder. It wasn't just growing louder as if she were getting closer; it was the snarling of famished animals whose hunger was building with anticipation.

Wolves? But Claire shook her head. She couldn't recall hearing such growling in the woods before. Or anywhere.

The noise skipped into savage roars, and Claire knew the animals were close. She craned her neck, but the shrubbery blocked her view. Clutching the weapon in a firm grip, she tiptoed over and peeked through the bushes.

A short distance away, Lance was seated on the ground, his back resting against a tree, as five wraith-like beasts stood around him, their mouths burrowing into his body.

Claire froze in shock, her body rigid, and a scream caught in her throat. The creatures—half-shadow, half-reptile—had smoky slivers swaying over their vaporous outlines as they unhurriedly savored their meal. As they feasted, portions of their shadowy halves solidified into thick, sooty scales.

Claire gawped with horror as their miasmic forms condensed into enormous, horned reptiles—dark as ebony, bigger than horses, long, bloody fangs glistening under their eyes of red flames.

Chills crawled down Claire's spine. The creatures appeared to have emerged from the ugliest depths of some nightmare. It wasn't just their appearance that evoked terror; there was something uncanny about the very presence of those beasts. Something so dark, even the insects of the night seemed to have shrunk into silent, motionless leaves, cowering as if in dread of the wind rising.

The strapping jaws of the creatures crunched on Lance's bones in the ghostly silence of the woods and Claire watched, horror dissipating her thoughts. The lantern lay on the grass beside the tree, and, in its light, she saw Lance blink. Her stomach tightened at once. Pulling herself together, Claire blazed out of the bush, pointed the muzzle at the pack and squeezed the trigger. The firearm rang out. One of the animals twitched a little, looked up at Claire, and then focused back on its meal.

Claire failed to believe her eyes.

Lance's head turned. He reached out, his hand trembling. Strips of torn flesh dangled from his elbow, swaying with the movement. "Help me…" he mumbled, blood spilling from his mouth with each word.

She took aim and fired again. The bullet struck another beast between the eyes and bounced away, like a drop of rain on a rock. Unhurt, the creature stared at her, entrails sticking out from between its fangs.

"Demons!" murmured Claire.

The beast ripped the other end of the intestine from Lance's belly and spread out its forelimbs into a pair of large, ribbed wings spanning at least ten arm lengths end-to-end, their serrated edges looking sharp as saws.

Claire loaded the rifle, her hands trembling.

The animal leaped off the ground, gliding over to her.

Claire glanced around, looked up at the sky, desperately begging for a miracle; begging for the emerald light to show up again. But something told her these terrible creatures could be stopped by no power on Earth.

Her throat dried, but she forced a long breath through her lungs. Finger on the trigger, she met the beast's stare as it chewed, unhurried, on its kill.

Her rifle blared and the animal's face jerked back as its right canine shot out and clattered against a tree.

A low growl spilled through its gnashing teeth. And then, rising up on hind legs, the reptile gave out a bellow, the veins on its sinewy chest jutting out as it roared.

Claire felt the ground under her shake. She fired again and watched the bullet bounce off its abdominal muscles.

The animal sprang at her and hacked at the rifle with its forelimb, smashing the muzzle. Claire drew back. It charged at her again. She seized the stock and barrel, planting the gun before her face and waiting for the blow to land. The beast struck the weapon, sawing it in two like a dead twig. And in the next moment, a flare of harrowing pain stormed through Claire's body, as sharp talons slashed across her shoulder. She fell to the ground with a cry.

The reptile placed its forelimb on her throat, sticky threads of blood and drool trickling down from its razor-sharp teeth, and sloughing down Claire's cheek.

"Go to hell, fucker," she seethed through the pain.

It raked along her body again, and for a moment Claire braced—then realized the claws hadn't broken the skin this time. The creature was snuffling her, its scaly nostrils scraping down her stomach. Claire lay under its weight, unable to move, its paw holding her fast as it dragged its snout lower across her abdomen.

Strength failing, Claire kept smacking at its foot with her fist, but the weight did not budge.

Cold, pointy claws sliced through her uniform.

She drew her foot up to the knife tucked in her shoe, but it teased her outstretched fingers—only a couple of inches away. With a jerk she twisted, trying to close the gap, and the sudden pull on her arm made the wound in her shoulder scream.

A harrowing cry rose from her throat, then fizzled. Her hand went limp. As her vision dissolved into haze, a pale flash of light flickered through the blur. And just before she sank into darkness, the last thing her failing senses caught was a sickening touch snaking beneath her torn uniform.

***

Tim trudged through the bushes, the firearm clenched in his grip. His instincts told him he would need it soon.

In fact, his instincts told him many things—that the worst had happened to the chancellor, that his comrades were in grave danger, that something was awfully wrong nearby. But Tim couldn't tell whether these warnings came from instincts or from fear. He tried to ignore them; those images of tragedy—visions he didn't even know were true—only weakened him. And he needed his courage to face whatever lay ahead.

Suddenly, a faint sound drifted to his ears—a steady chomping.

What on earth? Tim followed the sound quietly.

Cutting a pine tree, he picked his way through a marshy patch with furtive steps and pushed aside the branches. It offered a glimpse into the clearing ahead. Tim flinched with a shudder. The horror struck him like a sudden gust—chilling, sickening, stomach-churning. He drew back, eyes wide, jaw hanging.

His first impulse was to run, but his legs refused to obey. His wits froze, but his conscience hammered inside his head, urging him to act—to help his fellow soldiers, who had very little time.

Battling the wave of paralyzing fear with every shred of his strength, Tim gripped the firearm tightly.

"Oh Lord." He traced a cross over his chest. "Protect me from the devil—and his army."

***

A gun blared nearby, and a bestial cry of pain tore apart the silence. Claire awoke slowly, disoriented, the gunshot echoing in her ears like a shrill ringing.

Through the blur in her eyes, she watched a fuzzy outline slump on the ground beside her.

She turned, trying to gather her thoughts. Agony stabbed her body like a thousand sharp daggers with every movement. The creature seemed to have scraped her raw wherever it pleased— probably meaning to inflict the greatest possible torture before eventually killing her.

Claire turned her head to the other side. Silhouetted beneath the trees stood four creatures, just as before. But they were no longer focused on Lance—or whatever was left of him. Their gazes fixed on the trees in the distance, as if searching.

The firearm rang out again, and one of the four beasts jerked—slightly, the only sign of damage from the bullet. Then they abandoned their half-finished meal and scurried toward the muzzle flash.

Claire glanced at the animal beside her—it was squirming on the ground, a gunshot wound gaping in its spine—and then turned to Lance.

She pushed herself up, gritting her teeth, biting through the barbs of excruciating pain, and lurched toward him.

Lance's gaze was fixed on the ground, his torso a grotesque mass of torn flesh and mangled bone. Claire stroked her thumbs over his eyes, closing them, then looked toward the trees where the beasts had vanished.

Drawing the blade from her shoe, she staggered over to the injured creature. It lay as before, wheezing. She raised the knife, aiming for the bloody hole in its back—but stopped, eyes wide. The wound was closing, healing before her eyes.

In the distance, Tim's rifle cracked one last time, followed by his mortal cries echoing through the woods.

Claire turned helplessly toward the sound.

His screams were swallowed by the crunch of bones, the tearing of flesh, the guttural growls of the beasts.

Tears stung her eyes, but she forced them back. Tim could not be saved. The beasts would come for her next. Time was running out.

Claire staggered toward the valley, traces of orange dawn in the east guiding her through the uncharted woods.

CHAPTER 5

Arthur was surveying the area, his square warrior's face expressionless. The place had been secured by his soldiers, who remained standing around the carriage with firearms, as if there were something valuable left to guard. Arthur watched as Herbert trotted up to him.

Herbert stepped down from his horse, dragging himself to the chancellor's carriage, his sickly face and black pouches under his eyes screaming prolonged illness. He walked in slow, senile steps, and if not for the scar on his neck, it would have been hard to tell he was once a soldier.

"What a disaster!" Herbert shook his head.

"Not to worry, sir," Arthur reassured him. "I have sent in our men. They should be back soon."

"How long has it been?"

"Three hours, sir"

"And you are standing here doing *nothing*?" Herbert reprimanded him.

"Well..." Arthur hesitated. "The forest is vast, sir. Searching without getting lost is not easy."

"Which is why you need to send in *more* men, Major."

Arthur was going to say something but stopped. Herbert had already started moving up the trail of trampled shrubs into the woods.

Arthur came rushing after him. "It wouldn't be safe to go in there, sir."

"What bad can possibly happen in daylight?" Herbert ignored the warning and followed the footfalls.

Arthur realized it was useless to try to stop him. He gestured at two of the soldiers nearby. They nodded in compliance and tagged along with the elderly commander-in-chief.

Arthur waited for them to disappear behind the trees, straining to conceal the annoyance in his face.

"Was it really necessary to send those soldiers with the sick old man?"

Arthur shot a disapproving look at his subordinate, Nathan. "That *sick old man* has been heading regiments since before you were born, Sergeant."

"All the more reason to declare him useless." A snigger lit up the lanky fellow's weasel face. "The man is dying anyway."

"Watch it, Sergeant."

"Alright, alright." Nathan raised his hands in defense. "I am just saying, if you hadn't sent those soldiers with him, you'd probably be filling up the vacant commander-in-chief's position by tomorrow. There are wild animals in the woods, you know." He winked.

Arthur stared at him with cold eyes.

"Let's face it," Nathan went on, the smirk back on his lips. "He doesn't run the show anymore. So why let a title on paper keep you away from your worth? Food for thought." He marched off without waiting for a response.

CHAPTER 6

Deep in the woods, Herbert was huffing up the hill, his eyes sweeping through the bushes as he moved.

Suddenly, he stopped short. Claire lay beneath a tree. Herbert hurried forward, then froze beside her, taking in the shredded uniform, the ruin of her body. For a moment he only looked at her, lips pressed tight, before tugging the remnants of fabric across her as best he could.

"I found her!" he called over his shoulder.

The soldiers came running.

The old man pressed his fingers to her neck. "She's alive."

"Let's take her to the infirmary," one of the soldiers said.

The others gathered around Claire and began to lift her.

"Wait." Herbert studied the ruin of her body, his gaze lingering on the gaping wound in her shoulder, before saying, "Tell the Major to send in more men. Looks like we are up against some really nasty animals."

CHAPTER 7

Starting from the mountains in the north to the coastline in the south, the Company's dominion sprawled across the entire land. The local rulers had been thrown out of power nearly three decades ago. Ever since, the country had seen some unprecedented developments—roads were tarred, the importance of harbors increased, and trade and commerce had boomed. The army garrisons saw reinforcements now and then, with major grants allotted for the training of conscripted men and women. Witchcraft of all forms had been banned, the punishment for even associating with witches being death.

Life, however, did not change much for commoners. The picture on the streets changed from the King's men in blue roaming with swords to the Company's soldiers in red riding with firearms. The millers worked as before, as did the farmers, plague doctors, rat catchers, artisans, fishermen, apothecaries, and every other trade that had existed before. For them, the difference amounted to one thing they truly cared about—heavier taxes.

It was no different in Winsden. Flung far into the foothills of the mountains, it was just another place under the Company's rule, with a large public square, small thatched-roof houses, and business establishments dotting the skyline with smoking chimneys.

A road ran west from the public square and curved into a chaotic odor of freshly baked bread, slaughtered meat, fermenting grapes, and dirty laundry. Emerging out of the vibrant business neighborhood, the path turned north, running through the tranquility of birch and rosewood, and ending at a massive iron gate under a hill. From there, a narrow path curled up the slope to the doorway of a medieval castle—currently, the Company's army base in the district. Skirted by a dried moat around its thick concrete wall, the imposing structure sat like an eagle on a hilltop with its beak pointing at the sky.

A day had passed since the incident of the chancellor in the woods. Arthur was standing at the north tower window of the castle, soaking in the crisp fall breeze. The lavender sky of evening gazed down through sprays of yellow. The air smelled of jasmine, but still Arthur's mind refused to calm.

"Tough day?"

Arthur felt the brush of soft fingers on his arm. He turned. Rosaline stood behind him, dressed in a purple evening gown with a flowing skirt and a frilled bodice.

"You look magnificent." He forced a smile and then looked back out of the window.

Rosaline tucked her fingers between his. "Stop acting like you could have done something about it, please."

Arthur remained gazing absently at a hawk gliding through the sky. "The remains we buried were ghastly," he mumbled. "I have fought in many battles, Rozy. Seen death in many forms. But this was...this was something else."

"That's because they were killed by animals, not bullets."

"No." He shook his head. "It's not that. No animal I know of is capable of this." He paused for a moment. "The townspeople keep talking about demons in those woods. A fisherman disappeared last month. Bodies of woodcutters found two winters ago. Lumbermen who never returned. But we hardly ever stop to hear the woes of our people, let alone verify if their stories have any truth. Because...well, they are just stories that don't concern *us*."

"Demons or not, you did write to the chancellor asking him not to take the woods on his way to Winsden. So, it is not your burden to bear, Artie."

"Even if it is, I can live with that." Arthur turned to Rosaline. "But right now, it's something way bigger worrying me."

CHAPTER 8

Lines of white tombstones stood in gloomy silence against the rays of departing daylight. The place reeked of morbid emptiness. The same emptiness that was left in Dawn's heart. She remained seated on the grass, unmoving as a rock, her soft, delicate features pale. There was a desperate yearning in her pained eyes as she stared at the bed of loose earth, as if hoping her husband would climb out of it at any moment.

Not that she hadn't foreseen the possibility of this day when she had married a soldier, it was just that she had never thought it would be this way. They said a soldier's death in a battle meant glory. But this was no battle. This was not even fate. This was black magic.

The more Dawn thought about it, the more rage swelled in her heart. Her gullible husband had been tricked, and she would avenge him by any means necessary.

Black magic was forbidden in the land. Dawn recalled the hanging bodies at the public square following the days of trials of sorcerers.

Dawn swore by her dead husband's name that she would expose his killer, no matter the price.

CHAPTER 9

In one of the snug chambers within the inner quarters of the castle, logs crackled in the fireplace and gas lamps hung from small, inornate chandeliers. A hollow, full-body armor remained stationed by the door over a wooden pedestal, head slightly bowed, and the sword tip pinned between the feet in a compliant stance.

Herbert sat in a recliner by the fireplace. Arthur stood beside him, watching the old man warming his feet.

"Demons?" Herbert frowned. "That's outrageous!"

Arthur started to speak. "People in the town believe—"

"I don't care what they believe."

"We rule this country, sir." Arthur's tone was firm, but respectful. "The safety of its people is *our* responsibility."

"Then forbid them from entering the forest."

Arthur calmed himself down before replying to the ridiculous proposition. "That will be as good as taking the livelihood away from half the town, sir."

"So, what are you suggesting?"

"That the demons be slain."

Herbert regarded him for a moment. "My dear, Arthur," he said, his tone condescending. "If you stick to the outlandish and ludicrous story of demons, your battle is lost before it's even started. You want to make the woods safe for people—I understand that—but remember, minds filled with fear yield sooner to defeat. Your soldiers will fall prey to fear of demons that don't exist much before they fall prey to wild animals."

Arthur gave out a sigh, his mind unable to disagree with the idea. "In that case," he said, "I'll keep my thoughts to myself."

"Then what exactly will you tell your platoon?" asked Herbert.

"I... uhmm... I haven't thought of it yet."

"And," the old man said, his tone wry with sarcasm. "When do you propose to carry out this plan of sending Company troops to kill '*wild animals*' in the woods?"

Macabre images of corpses flashed before Arthur's eyes. "I won't send the troops, sir." His face turned stoney, his tone resolute. "I will lead them *myself.* Tonight."

CHAPTER 10

Bright light flooded Claire's vision.

"So." An indistinct outline floated over her face. "You are awake at last," a gruff male voice said.

"Wh-what happened?" Claire murmured, her head foggy.

"You survived," the doctor said softly. "The others didn't."

As her vision cleared, the blur sharpened into a tiny room with a narrow bed, a side table cluttered with vials and pill bottles, and a big, middle-aged man leaning over her.

"I need a horse," Claire said, pushing herself up.

"What are you doing?" the doctor cried. "You need to rest."

"A horse!" She glared at him.

He folded his arms, wary. "You're in no state to ride," he said, but after a beat he sighed. "Fine. If you insist—my horse is out back. Don't say I didn't warn you." Claire hobbled off the bed, grabbed a coat from the dresser and lurched through the doorway.

CHAPTER 11

The castle gazed up at the twinkling stars, strong winds hammering against its stone walls and drowning the whinnies from the stables. Clouds wafted around the towers, allowing the moon to flicker across the courtyard, where four dozen men and women were standing in squad formation.

Usually, formal meetings were convened during the day, and everyone was waiting to find out the reason for this exception.

Arthur closed his eyes and went through it for the fourth time. All his thoughts seemed to be in place. Yet, he was uneasy, for the elaborate narrative he had chalked in his mind for his soldiers was built upon one thing he hated: a lie. Reminding himself he had no choice, Arthur marched out to address his platoon.

He pointed at the Company flag waving on the barbican. "That...is not just a color of conquest. It is a promise of safety...of protection...of *every single thing* we owed the chancellor once he stepped into the district of Winsden." His voice a melancholy timbre, he continued. "And of everything we failed to offer him."

He looked at the faces for reactions. There were none.

"Well, *that* changes tonight," he continued. "The horrors of Thursday will never repeat for anyone—be it a soldier at home or a high-ranking guest from elsewhere."

This time, there was a murmur in the crowd.

"You may have heard stories..." Arthur decided to take the ripples of doubt head-on. "Stories about what's in those woods. Let me tell you—they are *not* true." Arthur fought to inject credibility into his words. "The townspeople made them up to scare their children...to distract us from the real demons—the *witches and sorcerers among them*."

The murmuring escalated.

"We cannot fight witches," Arthur continued. "So we strip them of their powers and execute them. But we *can* fight animals. Animals that took the lives of the chancellor, of Lance, of Tim, and the unfortunate coachman. And we *will* kill those man-eaters. *Tonight*."

The soldiers glanced at each other, some nodding, some shaking their heads.

"Any questions?"

Everyone was quiet for a moment, then one of the young cadets asked, "What kind of man-eaters are we expected to hunt down, Major?"

Arthur didn't know how to answer. "Well—"

"Flying reptiles!"

All heads turned.

From the side of the gatehouse, Claire limped across the courtyard, scars slanting across her pale ghostly face, and her shoulder swollen from the bandages under the long overcoat. "Enormous, ferocious, unkillable reptiles!"

The murmur escalated into an anxious chatter.

Arthur raised his hand. "SILENCE!"

The hum reduced but did not subside completely.

"What do you mean?" Arthur snarled.

"Bullets can't pierce their bodies." Claire moved past the soldiers and staggered up to the front. "No wound can kill them."

"Oh, yeah?" Arthur forced a mocking note into his voice.

"Those creatures"—Claire sank to her knees, panting—"are the emissaries of the devil himself."

"If that's true," Arthur said, glaring at her, mindful of the platoon's reactions to her statements. "What caused the devil to spare *you*?"

"I-I…" Claire stuttered.

"I'll tell you the reason."

All eyes turned to the gatehouse again. Lance's widow marched into the moonlight.

Dawn strode with purpose, her eyes daggers. "Claire lay in the woods for hours—*wounded, defenseless*. And the animals didn't kill her. *Why*?" She moved through the crowd, addressing the soldiers. "Because the devil doesn't live in the animals of the woods." She pointed at Claire. "It lives in *her*."

Claire looked up, aghast.

"Just think about it," Dawn went on, hysterical. "What animal in your knowledge is capable of such savagery?"

Confounded eyes stared at Claire, and Arthur watched quietly.

"You can't think of any, because there is none! It was no animal. It was *her* who killed my husband and the others," Dawn spluttered. "Claire is a *witch!*"

Arthur just stood there, a spectator. It didn't matter to him whether the allegations were true or not. All he cared about was that the angry widow's rants suited his own narrative. It would distract the soldiers from believing demons roamed the woods.

"Don't you see it?" Dawn cried. "That woman is a freak—an abomination to the natural order of things. She sleeps with another woman, because men are her food. I say we burn her at the stake this instant."

"*Enough!*" Herbert's roar echoed against the stone walls as he stomped into the area, silencing the grumble.

The old man walked over to the seething widow.

"I would have thrown you in the dungeons for the slanderous accusation you just leveled against a decorated soldier of the Company," Herbert growled, his voice iron, "but I forgive you this time because you are blinded to reason by grief. Sergeant!"

The sergeant appeared before the commander-in-chief and bowed.

"Show her out to the gatehouse," Herbert commanded and turned to Claire, who was hunched on her knees, gasping.

Herbert tried to help her rise, but Claire's eyes were glazed. "There were angels there," she managed with raspy breaths. "The sky turned green and winged angels came down to help...beautiful, fairy-like angels. But the beasts..."

Herbert sighed. He stroked Claire's head affectionately and called out, "Robin, escort her to her home. She needs rest."

***

Nathan ushered the distraught widow to the outer gate of the castle. Dawn walked like a defeated warrior, gaze lowered, shoulders slumped.

"Lance was a brother to me," Nathan mumbled.

Dawn did not speak.

"It pains me to see his widow turned away, empty-handed." Nathan paused before adding, "I want to ask you something."

Dawn glanced at him, lips trembling.

"Are you sure of everything you said back there?" Nathan's tone suggested he was ready to act at one nod from her. "About Claire?"

"Yes." Dawn's eyes lit up. "Yes!"

Nathan said nothing. He quietly led her through the gatehouse.

When they were out in the open, he looked around.

"In that case—" Nathan was certain the guards were too far away to hear him. "I will see to it Lance's murderer gets the punishment she deserves."

"I..." Dawn's voice was shaking. "I want her to burn."

"Then burn she will." Nathan touched her hand lightly. "You have my word."

Dawn clenched his hand, her eyes welling up.

Three guards cantered up to the gate, glancing at the two as they rode past.

"You may leave now." Nathan was conscious of the curious eyes.

Dawn turned, and as she ambled down the hill, Nathan watched her departing form.

The foundation had been laid. Nathan grinned, imagining Dawn naked in bed under him.

CHAPTER 12

The northwestern part of the town had a sprawling scatter of small houses. The colonies were furrowed by narrow, compact lanes, dotted with business enterprises—potters, furniture-sellers, smiths, craftsmen. The area was inhabited by families from diverse walks, and yet a sense of solidarity bound them. Everyone was for everyone else, and the reason for the unity was the fact no particular profession dominated.

It was long past the working hours of the day, and the crowds in the lanes had thinned down. However, the group of men and women outside Alice's door were in no rush to return to their homes. Faces clouded with anxiety, they loitered.

The miller's son came running along the path. "She's coming," he shouted, pointing at the carriage rattling behind him.

Dressed in peasant's attire, Alice—a sturdy, middle-aged woman with a warm, friendly face now drawn with distress—hurried from the house at once.

The horses stopped, and the carriage door swung open. The crowd rushed to help Claire inside, their anxious voices rising in near chorus.

"She looks so pale."

"I will ready the broth."

"Take her to bed."

"Be careful."

"Get her some good rest, will you?" Robin told Alice before the carriage drove away.

They laid her on the bed and tucked the pillows to her side.

Five minutes later, Alice latched the door behind the last neighbor.

"I went to the Company infirmary," she said, sitting by Claire's bedside. "The doctor said you ignored his advice and left." She suddenly yelled in frustration, "What the hell's wrong with you?"

Claire shrugged. "I am fine. Don't worry."

"Your lies won't work on me, girl." Alice stared at her with stern eyes.

"Relax, Al," Claire complained. "It's just a gash in my shoulder. Nothing else."

"You better be right about that *'nothing else'*." Alice started unbuttoning Claire's coat, her eyes scanning her body. "Haven't been able to look at you properly since they brought you from the woods."

Alice removed the coat. Claire's body was mottled with small cuts and bruises, and the dressing on her shoulder hung partly undone. Alice's brows arched, her eyes widening.

"Come now, Al," Claire stopped her before another round of scolding could begin. "They're just nicks."

Alice's jaw tightened. She seemed ready to snap but held herself back with visible effort. "What was it?" She asked at last. "The animal?"

Claire gave no reply.

Alice began to peel away the bandages from her shoulder, then stopped midway, horror flashing across her face. Tears welled in her eyes. She squeezed them shut and turned away. "Good Lord!"

Claire caught her shudder. "I am alive, Al," she said, threading her fingers through Alice's. "The others weren't that lucky."

Alice steadied herself, her face struggling to resume her usual mask of hardness. "I'll have Walton change this after your bath. He'll be here any moment, with his… stuff." Her hands were tender but her expression twisted into a grimace as the wound came fully into view—three curving fissures of clawed flesh, the central one deeper.

"Was it a bear?" She fixed Claire with a stare at her.

Claire stayed silent.

Alice searched her face. "What happened at the castle?"

She dropped her gaze.

"Why did you go there, girl? What was so urgent?"

Claire remained silent, hesitation flickering in her eyes.

"I deserve to know," Alice snapped.

Claire exhaled a weary sigh. "I don't want you thinking I'm crazy."

"Try me."

Claire shrugged. "Creatures of the dark chased off a host of angels, killed my men, and slobbered over me. What do you think?"

Alice didn't answer.

Claire waited. But Alice only began to remove Claire's clothes, avoiding her gaze. "Let's give you a bath," she said coldly.

The impassive note in Alice's voice stung. Claire recalled the pity in the commander-in-chief's face. Deep down, she had thought Alice, of all people, would believe her.

With sagging spirit, she let Alice guide her to the tub. The hot water lapped the cramped muscles in her worn-out body, but somehow it brought no comfort to her.

Neither spoke for a while. Alice bathed her, gingerly cleaning the wounds.

"People fear what they don't understand," Alice slowly said after a pause. "They'd rather take you for a lunatic than face the existence of unknown horrors around them. After all, dark legends of demons do circulate in town, but the truth is, no one has ever escaped them and lived to tell the tale."

Claire stared at her, surprised.

Alice helped her out of the tub. "I would have trusted you, girl, even if you'd told me a make-believe story." She patted Claire dry with a cloth, helped her into a fresh night smock and tucked her into bed.

"So"—Claire hesitated—"you believe me because I want you to?"

There was a tap on the door.

"You wanting me to is a reason good enough for me to believe anything, baby." Alice pulled the blanket over Claire and went to answer the door.

A man with white, silken hair and a chest-long beard, stumbled inside, bent with age, a smoldering cauldron clutched in his hands.

Shuffling into the room, he plonked the cauldron by the bedside. "Feed this broth to her," he instructed Alice. "And the girl will be racing like a horse by midnight."

"Stop exaggerating, Walton."

"I never exaggerate." His voice was steel.

"Whatever you say, old man. Now patch her up, will you?" Alice handed him a pile of clean bandages, cotton, and antiseptic.

"Let me see it."

Claire parted her nightgown just enough to expose her shoulder.

The apothecary sterilized the wound and began dressing it. As Claire winced, the fabric slipped from her grip and slid lower. The old man's glance flicked her chest. Her hand shot up in reflex to cover herself, but Walton caught her wrist and leaned over her.

"What do you think you're—?" Alice started to growl.

Walton raised his hand with finality, silencing her.

Claire was taken aback as a strange aura came over the old man, making it impossible for her to defy him.

He tugged the gown down farther, and for some reason, she couldn't object.

"Dragons," he muttered, brooding as he traced the faint claw marks on her skin.

"What?" Alice asked.

"Dragons," he repeated, letting go of Claire's wrist. "Not myths. Real creatures."

Claire covered herself, her mind reeling.

"And you could tell that from those marks?" Alice's voice carried incredulity.

"The corpses they buried this morning were those beasts' hunger. This"—he pointed at Claire's shoulder—"is their rage. And the marks across the rest of you are their lust. You can't mistake these for the marks of an ordinary animal."

Alice and Claire exchanged glances.

"Well, even if dragons do exist, they're just another animal… like, I don't know, overgrown lizards or crocodiles or something," Alice said.

"Reptiles," Claire quietly corrected.

"Yes, right. Reptiles. But you speak of them as if they're like humans?"

"If that is the impression I gave you, let me correct myself," Walton replied. "Dragons are nothing like humans. They're far superior in every way. Their strength is near godlike, as are their powers."

The women exchanged another glance.

"Even if I believe that absurd story, how do you explain the lust? I mean a crocodile births a crocodile; a human births a human. But you expect me to believe that they—those reptiles—lusted after my Claire, a human? It doesn't make sense. How are dragons even born?"

Walton paused, his frail frame wobbling as he sighed. "From the darkest of curses."

Claire eyed him for a long moment. "Tell me everything you know about them," she said.

"I already have." Walton hastily tied the last knot on the bandage and rose from his seat. Suddenly, he seemed eager to leave.

"Please!" Claire urged. "Those monstrosities killed my men. Good men. Brave soldiers…" her voice trailed off, heavy with grief.

Walton was halfway to the door when he stopped.

"One of the widows thinks I am a witch who devoured her husband—and the others."

Walton slowly turned.

"It may not take long for everyone else to see it that way." Claire's voice broke as she begged him for direction. "Please, I need answers."

"So you seek answers not because you want to know what killed your men, but because you fear for yourself?"

Claire lowered her gaze. "I am asking for your help, Walton. Think of the reason however you like."

The age-withered apothecary heaved a sigh. "Find Gertrude Smith in Lockewall—if she is still alive. But know this: not every answer is meant to be sought. Nature keeps certain forces beyond the reach of humankind. It's a balance that must never be disturbed. Never."

Walton left, the door closing behind him, and the women stood staring in his wake.

CHAPTER 13

Rosaline hurried down the corridor and ran into Herbert's chamber. "Father?"

The old man squirmed in his recliner, possessed by a vicious spasm of coughing.

"Mary!" Rosaline darted to her father as he collapsed on the floor.

The maid sprinted in.

"Get his pills." Rosaline held Herbert up, his frail frame juddering in her arms with each convulsive burst of wheezing. It looked as if he would fall apart any moment. She stroked his head, massaged his back, rubbed his chest—desperate, unable to tell what would help.

The maid returned with the medicines.

Rosaline kept on trying everything her instincts suggested, and a few minutes later, she could tell the worst of the storm had blown over. At least for the moment. The hawking still persisted, but it was less nasty.

She eased Herbert back into the recliner and held out a pill. "Take this."

Herbert pushed it away and waved at the maid to leave. Mary hesitated, and then bowed and withdrew.

"Medicines do no good now," Herbert wheezed.

Rosaline stared at him. There was an unpleasant note in his words—a note of finality, a note of surrender, a note of truth.

"What do you mean?"

"It has spread everywhere. I can sense it." Herbert took the mug of hot beverage from the side table and his gaze fell absently on the hearth. The flame reflected in his eyes, contrasting with their dreariness.

Rosaline kept staring at the frail figure, recalling how she had grown up playing in his big, strong arms, toying with the glittery medals studding his bright, red uniform.

She remembered the charismatic faces waiting at the lobby to speak to him—people of rank, with sharp eyes and brawny physiques, who approached her father with respect, sought his opinion, and nodded at his advice. His vitality had once been so intense that, watching him in action, Rosaline could almost feel his aura of strength against her skin.

When he returned home, she would look into the battle-hardened face of the tough, intimidating commander and be amazed at how she would find a soft, adoring man in there.

Her father was a fountain of life—a fountain that had always bubbled against every difficulty, until this incurable disease had slowly drained it dry. She knew the illness had withered his body, but she'd never seen his spirit bow to it—not until this very moment. And more than the thought of him gone, it was this air of resignation about him that shattered her.

"Don't say that, Father," she mewled. "We'll call the best physicians in the country."

Herbert took a sip from the mug. A crimson tint dripped down the edge of the white ceramic. "You can do as you please, my dear," he said, taking her hand. "But promise me not to expect miracles, for I cannot bear to see you with your hopes dashed, no matter where I am."

Rosaline looked at him, wishing to hide her face into his chest the way she used to when she was a little girl. But nothing would hurt him more than the expression of her weakness, and Rosaline knew it.

"If you say so, Father." She stepped out of the room with a straight face, ran into her chamber, and broke into tears.

CHAPTER 14

It had been an hour since Claire left. She'd talked Alice into letting her go by herself. And Alice cursed herself for allowing it. Walton's herb-infused concoction had turned out to be really potent—in fact, a bit too potent.

What if she fainted on the way?

What if she got lost in the woods?

What if...?

Wriggling in the bed, Alice didn't realize when the kaleidoscope of disturbing thoughts in her mind solidified into a continuous vision: Claire was riding down the treeline of a hill, the sky above a swirling sea of molten tar that spewed out angry Company soldiers. Midair, the men twisted into gigantic, flying reptiles that chased Claire with drooling mouths. One of them glided across and struck her, hurling her to the ground. The pack leaped upon her, tearing her clothes apart. Then smoke rose from the grass, coiling upward in thick volumes, and the dragons dissolved back into naked human soldiers who collapsed, rasping.

Alice woke to a fit of coughing. The room was choked with smoke that reeked of burning wood. Disoriented, she looked around. Through the black haze, she saw flames—dancing, raging flames.

Alice peeled herself off the bed, her head spinning. Faint screams seeped into her ears beneath the constant crackling of wood.

She lurched toward the door, but her foot caught on something and she crashed to the floor with a thud. Searing pain jolted through her skull.

The screams outside became Claire's voices—dozens of them—screaming, distorting, overlapping.

"Claire?" Alice clawed through the haze with renewed vigor, groping blindly. Warm fluid trickled down her forehead, but she refused to give up. "I'm coming."

Fatigue pressed in on her, thick and steady, like the press of storm clouds blocking the last traces of sunlight. But Alice pushed on—ignoring it—towards the only thing that mattered, blood partially blinding her left eye.

Claire seemed to be calling out Alice's name, her voices trailing, echoing, fading like she was moving away.

"Wait." Head heavy as a rock, Alice stretched out her arm in a desperate yearning, as if to touch the fleeting sound of Claire's voices with her palm. "Don't go."

With a loud crack, a burning log came crashing down from the roof.

CHAPTER 15

The cloud of dirt raced through the fog, dismantling the silence of the woods with the clopping of hooves—hundreds of them. Soldiers galloped as spirits of the night, raging down the path under a cloak of mist.

Suddenly, a light flickered across the eastern sky like an ornate lamp stifled behind a curtain.

Arthur, leading the squad, gazed up at it.

The sky turned green...

Claire's words flashed in his mind. No matter what Arthur had said to manipulate his men, he had not disbelieved her entirely, which was why he couldn't shake the feeling of unease at the pit of his stomach.

Arthur sighed, thankful not many had heard Claire's barely audible mumbling in the castle's windy courtyard, or his task would have been a lot more difficult.

Peering at the eerie emerald glow through the fog, he had to remind himself he was entrenched by a squad of trained soldiers who were armed to the teeth. He had nothing to fear.

"To the east," Arthur roared, steering his horse off the path.

The others followed the major.

Erin cantered up to him. "Is it wise to stray from the objective, Major?" she asked.

"I don't think we are straying, Sergeant."

She looked at him, puzzled.

"What do you think that light is?"

"I have no idea," she conceded.

"Neither do I." Arthur grinned. "And that's what assures me we are on the right track."

"I..." she hesitated. "I don't quite follow."

"What do you do when you notice something peculiar, Sergeant?"

"I look into it."

Arthur beamed approvingly. "I believe that's precisely what the chancellor and our soldiers did on Thursday night."

Comprehension flashed on Erin's face. "And encountered the man-eaters on the way," she said, nodding.

"Watch your powder!" Arthur hollered as it started to drizzle.

The soldiers covered their ammunition.

The land sloped up to the east and the undergrowth was getting thicker as they ascended. Sounds of steady clip-clopping had reduced into the tired tapping of hooves under the pattering of raindrops.

"Should we wear out the horses, Major?" Erin said.

"It's either them or us," Arthur replied.

"I think we can be better equipped for a surprise attack if we are on foot."

"Your suggestion is noted, Sergeant."

Erin paused for a moment and then pulled back with the others.

The horses hobbled up the hill toward the chartreuse dash shimmering behind the fog.

Wilbur rode up to their leader. "What *is* that, Major?" he asked, peering at the sheen.

"We'll find out."

"And where will we set up the bait?"

"The right place."

"You mean where we found our soldiers… up there?"

Arthur stared at the young cadet's face. He noticed no offense, just the restless curiosity of a rookie

His horse's front leg sank into a bush, lurching him forward, and he leaped off instinctively.

The squad halted, watching as Arthur inspected the undergrowth.

"Leave your horses here," Arthur ordered, his gaze brushing over Erin's face. "We walk."

CHAPTER 16

The pale moonlight filtered through a single gargantuan oak tree that looked down on the only sign of human existence in the area—a decrepit hut at the side of a narrow path. Rays from a flickering lamp seeped through the cracks in the closed windows and dimly lit the dense overgrowth of wild shrubs hugging the shack.

Claire pulled on the reins. The place seemed to reek of despair.

Staking the horse, she held out her lantern and slowly moved toward the hut. Fresh chalk powder lay sprinkled on the ground. Claire crossed the chalk line and peered at the hut.

The mossy walls of the shack were scribbled with layers upon layers of graffitied curses and words of damnation like some unholy palimpsest.

She tapped on the door.

There was no answer.

"Madame Gertrude Smith?" She knocked again.

The door unlatched and parted a little to reveal a scrawny face furrowed with age and illness.

"Who are you?" the woman said in a weak voice.

Claire stared at the exhausted eyes that seemed drained of strength.

After her long journey, Claire had ridden through Lockewell's lanes for nearly an hour, trying to track down the old woman. The stories she'd heard hadn't painted Madame Smith in a good light. *That evil woman isn't allowed in Lockewall… She is a witch. She is a manifestation of the devil.*

Yet now, even the tiny part of her that had believed the townspeople could not connect this face with those stories. It wasn't the kind of face she'd seen at the gallows, condemned for practicing witchcraft. To Claire, this woman seemed nothing more than a harmless eccentric—perhaps one who knew a little more about the woods than the average commoner.

"Claire Hawkins. I'm a Company soldier, Madame."

"No one calls me that." Gertrude's eyes narrowed suspiciously. "What do you want?"

"Dragons." Claire got straight to the point. "Tell me about them."

A momentary flick of horror paled the already sickly face, but it disappeared the next instant under a dismissive look of sternness. "Get out of here!" she said, starting to shut the door.

"Wait!" Claire held the flimsy piece of wood. "Madame," she beseeched, softening her tone.

"I cannot help you, Claire Hawkins."

"Lives are at stake."

"They always are," Madame Smith said, her voice devoid of emotion. "If you are not here to burn me, then stop bothering me."

Claire recoiled, unsettled. It wasn't the indifference—it was the effortless certainty with which the old woman dismissed her, the unshakable authority in her voice. It was then Claire understood: this was indeed the Madame the townspeople had whispered about.

Realizing she was wasting time, Claire released the door.

It closed in her face.

***

As Gertrude engaged the latch, she drew away with a startled jolt. Her palm had accidentally brushed over the part of the wood Claire had touched.

Gertrude's trembling hand stretched out again to make sure. As her skin came in contact with the area, a bolt of electricity sizzled through her fingers.

Gertrude sank to the floor, her body shaking.

***

Claire staggered toward her horse—distracted, drained. Gertrude Smith was the only lead she had had… the lone straw she had tried to cling to in search of truth. The truth that could have saved her from a witch's fate. And it felt ridiculous that she gave up on that solitary ray of hope so easily. Was it exhaustion? Or had she, deep down, already given up even before leaving Winsden?

Her thoughts were broken by a rattling sound. Claire turned.

"Come on in, Claire Hawkins." It was more of a command than an invitation.

Claire blinked.

"I don't have all night."

Claire found herself plodding back to the door and stepping inside the old woman's home.

Logs to make fire, an earthen pot, berries and wild bean tubers spilling from a grubby straw basket in the corner, a threadbare rug curled up to the wall on the damp floor—everything inside was consistent with the ramshackle exterior. Everything, except one object—a block of stone at the side of the room which held some worn-out religious books next to a candle.

"Who sent you?" Gertrude asked.

Claire was staring at the books, pondering their oddness against the rest of the wretched shack, but she turned to face the old woman when she spoke.

"How much do you know about me?" the woman asked again, impatiently.

See Gertrude Smith in Lockewall... It hadn't even been a matter of hours since she had first heard the woman's name, but it felt like she'd been tracking her for months. Such was the power of a bad name in town, nobody wanted to miss out on filling a stranger in with embellished tales of misdeeds.

"Just enough to know you are the person I should see."

"And..." Madame Smith said slowly. "Why do you think you should see me?"

Claire paused for a moment to gather her thoughts. "There are dark powers in the woods, darker than anything I have seen, and I want to understand them."

Gertrude eyed Claire's left shoulder, puffed-up with bandages under her coat. "You survived them, didn't you?"

Claire didn't answer.

"How?"

"A soldier—a good man named Timothy Willis." Claire's voice was heavy.

"And he is...?"

Claire exhaled and shook her head.

Gertrude remained silent for a moment. She walked over to the window and pushed it open.

"It's a curse," she said at last, almost a whisper. "A punishment for a sin."

"What sin?"

Gertrude's eyes stilled as she gazed at the distant silhouettes of mountains piercing the starry sky, taking her mind back to where it all began. "Falling in love. Ophelia and Basil—two pure, young souls so much in love..." her twinkling eyes turned somber. "Love... that invited a dreadful curse."

Claire stared at her questioningly.

"A long time ago, divine creatures used to walk that place...wonderful, magical beings capable of great love and kindness toward humans.

"*But* not every kind of love was permitted, and Ophelia didn't understand that until it was too late. She fell in love with a mort—"

Gertrude cast a cautious glance at the door. "Lower the flame," she instructed, her tone suddenly alert.

She closed the window quickly, hobbled over to the door and put the latch on.

Claire could hear a distant commotion. "What's going on?"

"Nothing unusual"—Gertrude doused the other lantern—"once you've been branded a witch."

CHAPTER 17

The drizzle became rain.

Soaked to the skin, Arthur and his squad hiked up the hill, huddled into their jackets, their boots sinking into the mud as they plodded upward.

A green bolt of light shot across the eastern sky, stopping abruptly over them, and the party stumbled to a dazed standstill.

From that emerald blaze, a luminous white spilled forth, spiraling gently downward

The soldiers peered through the pouring rain as the light took on the outline of a winged woman descending into their midst, illuminating everything in celestial radiance.

"What are you all doing here?" she asked, her voice strained with concern.

Her shine slowly softened, revealing a face that could grace an idol. Strands of flowing, resplendent hair brushed across her porcelain skin. Her goddess-like body was bathed in a gentle halo of light.

Claire's voice played inside Arthur's head. *And winged angels came down to help...beautiful, fairy-like angels...*

"Don't you know this place is dangerous?" the angel asked.

The soldiers didn't speak. They didn't even move. They just stood there, mesmerized by her splendor.

"Who are you people?" She looked at the faces of the young men and women with anxious eyes.

Arthur threaded his way through the squad. "I am Major Arthur Ward of the Company's Fifteenth Infantry Regiment. And these soldiers are under my command." He stared at her suspiciously. "Who are *you*?"

The angel's soft smile exuded a warmth that seemed to soothe the very air around her. Her calm blue eyes gave out a kindness—an aura of affection—that made Arthur feel as if he were wrapped in a comforting embrace.

"I am"—her divine radiance faded, and her glowing skin dulled to a dead, ashen hue—"your destiny."

Her once-kind smile curled into a twisted grin that simmered with a deep, dreadful darkness. The gentle blue of her eyes flickered, becoming searing, amber flames that pulsed with a malevolent brilliance, making Arthur take a step back.

Wraithlike smoke seemed to throb from the earth around her, twisting upward in ribbons of obsidian that coiled and churned like a midnight maelstrom.

The soldiers drew back, too aghast to notice four more tufts of light had emerged from the ring right above them.

They stood frozen, watching as the darkness climbed the angel's body, swirling around her waist and rising higher in a writhing shroud of ebony strands. Through the whirl of blackness, they glimpsed her form twisting and distorting, godlike magnificence warping into hideous monstrosity.

When the vortex of shadows finally dispersed, the angel was gone. Towering in her place loomed a grotesque, winged reptile. Its scales gleamed with an oily sheen, and its eyes burned with savage, fiery intensity. The once-beautiful angelic wings had become vast, scraggy structures, their serrated edges sharp as blades.

CHAPTER 18

When the noises outside calmed, Gertrude raised the flame.

"Now you better get going, Claire Hawkins," she whispered, opening the door. "Your presence in my home will only support that widow's claim and put you at the end of a noose."

"Winsden is a good thirty miles away from here," Claire assured in an almost humorous tone. "Word from Lockewall can't travel that far."

The old woman stepped out with the lantern. Claire began to follow, but then stopped abruptly.

Gertrude glanced back. "Got attached to my palace already?"

Claire stared at her, brow furrowed. "How did you know about the widow's claim?"

Gertrude brushed off the question and, instead, shone her light on the wall. The words "*Rot in hell witch*" were written in fresh blood.

"Answer me," Claire snarled.

Gertrude's wrinkled fingers grazed over the scrawling on the wall. "At the core of every rumor," she mumbled, "there is often a trace of truth, Claire Hawkins." She moved over to the sprinkled chalk line and knelt down, her saddened eyes fixed on the bundle on the ground. "Well, not all rumors. I wonder who gave them the outrageous idea of throwing dead strays at a witch to reduce her powers." She started to collect the remains of the butchered cat.

Claire watched her. She had always believed witches, no matter how seemingly alike to humans, were threats. And coexistence could never be safe in the long run.

"How did you escape trial?" There was no sympathy in Claire's tone.

Instead of replying, Gertrude pointed at her window. "Hand me that rock, will you?"

Claire turned to the window. A palm-sized rock with a sharp edge lay on the sill. She picked it up and tossed it to Gertrude, wondering what trick the woman would have pulled off to dodge the law.

"The jury needed evidence to convict me." Gertrude took the rock and started digging a grave into the ground with its spade-like edge. "But they found none in my possession—no potion, no magical stone, no evidence to support any allegations of witchcraft."

"And they let you go?" Claire scowled with contempt. "Just like that?"

"The law isn't unfair, Claire Hawkins. You are innocent until proven guilty."

Claire had heard that witches often tried to suppress their powers to escape detection. As far as she knew, nearly all of them perished when the forcefully contained magic imploded. "You suppressed your magic for all these years," she said. "But how?"

Gertrude glanced at her. "No one can suppress magic for this long." Her eyes drifted away. "Not without becoming a destructive force capable of—" Getrude shook her head. "Never mind."

Claire studied her intently.

Gertrude's eyes shifted back to the unfortunate feline. She gave out a sigh. "I wish they'd stop killing these poor creatures."

The remark infuriated Claire. "They wouldn't have to if you hadn't tricked the jury at your trial." Her tone was filled with hate. "You *are* a witch, after all—a threat to the less powerful."

"And I thought all you cared about were the threats *darker* than witches." Gertrude laughed quietly. "I don't blame you, girl. Burning at the stake, drawing and quartering, feeding to the lions, impaling... Why would anyone torture a person so horribly, just to do something so basic as to take their life? It's because execution is a sport, Claire Hawkins. Watching others suffer gives one a certain joy, a feeling of power. The rallies of *'Burn the witch'* are more a barbaric desire to watch a woman suffer, than the wish for a society free of witches. It's innate in humans."

"That's not true," Claire protested.

"Oh, is it not?" The old woman smirked.

Claire tried to reply, but something deep inside her held her back. Images of the executions she had overseen at the public square coursed through her mind—the twitching of legs under the hanging bodies, the heads rolling down the blood-spattered stairs under a guillotine, and the cheer it drew from the crowd. Claire felt a jolting pang in her conscience. It was as if the old woman's statements carried an unpleasant ring of truth—that civilized society had chosen to hide behind a facade of 'strict punishment to set examples for wrongdoers.' A facade meant to preserve society's label of being 'civilized'.

Claire breathed a sigh. She wanted to probe further, but somehow, she couldn't make herself question the woman again. Claire turned to leave.

"That night when they made love in the woods," Gertrude began, "the curse struck them."

Claire turned back.

"Ophelia pushed her lover away, but Basil couldn't escape the horror. The ill-fated man watched the beautiful angel transform into an ugly, winged reptile under a bolt from the sky."

Claire gasped. "The angel transformed…"

Gertrude stared at her surprised face. "The angels *are* the dragons, Claire Hawkins. Cursed with a life of darkness. Their hunger can never be satisfied."

Claire felt gutted. How could this be true? She recalled the events of that fateful night, over and over, until, like a crack of lightning, she realized she'd never actually seen the fairy-like creatures fly *back* to the sky.

"Slowly, the curse spread to the other angels, for they were all connected by the same spirit," Gertrude continued. "It was tragic how those magnificent, glorious beings changed into such odious demons, one by one—all because of the sin committed by a single one of them." She paused, then added in a low, almost absent-minded soliloquy, "And yet the absence of that same sin would make the world fall apart. Ironic, isn't it?"

Claire was holding on to the trunk of the oak tree, processing. "How could something as pure and true as love have invited such a dreadful curse?" She asked after a moment.

Gertrude looked up, lost in her train of thoughts. "What?"

"It was just love between two young souls. Why was it forbidden?"

"Because human seed in an angel's womb yields an abomination—a creature of unspeakable horror, a creature of the netherworld. Ophelia knew that, and yet she could not hold herself back."

"Yes, I have heard of their lust," Claire pointed.

"Lust?" The old woman's already wrinkled forehead scrunched up further with surprise. "No. No, Claire Hawkins," she shook her head vehemently. "There was no lust in them. Their union, if allowed, would have created something demonic, but their feelings were divine. It was love… in the purest form you can think."

"And how do you know that?"

"You see," Gertrude held out her hand, explaining. "Lust is just a base instinct planted by nature to lure a creature towards another that promises superior offspring. And procreation between a male human and a female angel bears no such thing, which is why attraction of body between such a pair is insignificant. It's only love that can bring them close."

Claire frowned, the pieces refusing to add up in her head. "So angels don't lust over humans?"

"No, they do. A male angel is very likely to lust over… certain female humans."

"And why's that?"

"Well, their union produces a being that is part god and part human—a demigod with powers beyond any mortal's wildest imagination. But not every woman has the capacity to bear such a child. In fact, she won't even attract an angel's attention unless she possesses the right life force."

Claire was deep in thought. "Why such a grim disparity between the offspring of the two pairs?"

"Well, an unholy drop in a bucket of pure water makes the entire bucket impure, doesn't it?"

"I don't understand."

"It's simple, Claire Hawkins. Human womb is divine, but human seed is not."

Claire scoffed. "Quite unfair, isn't it?"

"How so?"

"You call human seed unholy, but can anything truly be unholier than what those angels have now become? They procreating a beast of the netherworld is understandable, but a demigod? I mean, what godly quality do those despicable creatures still retain?"

"None." Gertrude flattened the bed of the pit carefully with her hands, readying it before laying the animal there. "I wasn't talking about the creatures you met in the woods. The rules of procreation I just told you applied to pure, good-hearted angels… not to the hideous shape-shifters they became after the curse."

"And how do the rules apply to those hideous shape-shifters?"

"I don't know." A shudder of fright ran across Gertrude's face. "Nobody does. And you should pray it stays that way."

Gertrude closed her eyes and muttered a short, but solemn prayer. And Claire could not tell whether it was for the peace of the animal's soul whose remains she placed inside the pit or for the horror of the possibility she just imagined in her head.

Claire thought it best to change the subject. "What became of Basil?" she asked. "Did he return?"

Gertrude nodded. "But he too was scarred."

"What happened?"

The old woman became pensive. "It was long before the Company had taken over. Magic and sorcery used to be common gossip in public squares back then. The angels in the woods were no secret to anyone, and neither was what Basil had done. The king did not punish him, but the boy became an outcast in Lockewall, and he would remain so for as long as he lived."

Gertrude began covering the pit with earth, each fistful laid down with the tenderness one might show a loved one's grave.

"A week after the incident, they found Basil in a ditch in the eastern part of the woods. Sharp teeth and claw marks had shredded his corpse into an unrecognizable pulp." Gertrude gave out a sorrowful sigh. "It's ironic that the boy responsible for setting off the curse ended up becoming its first victim."

"Why did he go back to the woods?"

"Nobody knows. Nobody cares. It's been some fifty winters. No one even remembers him anymore." Gertrude touched her fingers to the small mound tenderly.

"If the curse has been there for that long, how come I didn't hear of it sooner?"

"You probably would have, if you paid any real attention to the lives of the people you rule over."

"What's that supposed to mean?"

"The townspeople today may not know the complete truth, but they are respectful of the words passed down from their ancestors, forbidding them from entering the eastern part of the woods. But despite that, mishaps happen at times. Some hot-headed woodcutter or absentminded fisherman would lose their way and end up in a dragon's belly once in a while."

The sight of Lance being ravenously devoured alive played before Claire's eyes. "You mean those beasts with their endless hunger have lived all these years on just a handful of men who wandered off, lured by their emerald light in the sky? That's maybe less than a dozen in fifty years."

"Don't forget the birds and the animals. Their hunger doesn't even spare snakes or insects—but those can't give them what humans can."

Claire didn't hear the last part. "I don't understand. Why lurk in the woods waiting for prey when they can storm into towns and take their fill?"

"An invisible cage holds them," Gertrude said. "A cage as old as the curse itself that is meant to contain the dragons in a small part of the woods so mankind can remain safe outside it."

"And this cage can hold them forever?"

"It is meant to, but..."

"But?" Claire gaped at Gertrude in horror. "But *what*, Madame?"

"When they feast on a human, they don't just take their body. They take their spark, their vitality."

"What are you saying?"

"The shield won't be able to hold them forever. The more human souls they take, the stronger they get. And sometime soon..." The old woman's voice shook. "There will be a catastrophe."

Claire sensed chills pulsing through her. She was thinking of the squad in the castle's courtyard where Arthur was talking about carrying out an assault tonight. She could taste the bile rising in her throat. Suddenly, this had become way bigger than the lives of a few soldiers. Claire darted to her horse, determined to stop them before it was too late, even though a part of her knew it was already too late.

"How do we kill them?" she demanded, hurling herself into the saddle.

"Shoot them through the heart, and it will weaken them for a while. But nothing I know of will kill them."

Claire remembered the dragon writhing in agony after Tim's bullet struck it in the back and pierced its heart.

She wondered how the witch's knowledge could be so frighteningly accurate. Perhaps it was true of all witches—there was nothing they didn't know when it came to dark powers. This was why they had to be eradicated. But it didn't matter now. *Right now,* the only thing she cared about was that there wasn't a second to lose.

She nudged the horse to move, but then, as she caught up with her thoughts, she pulled the reins to stop. "Where are Basil's parents?" she asked.

"Died many winters ago."

"Brothers… sisters…?"

"He was an only child and a lonely one." Gertrude paused broodingly for a moment. "But he did have a friend. His *only* friend. I haven't seen that boy since Basil's death."

"You remember his name?"

"Fraser," the old woman said. "Herbert Fraser."

CHAPTER 19

The rain had finally relented, leaving a clear, moonlit sky shining down on a grotesque tableau of horrors. Corpses lay strewn across the undergrowth—matted in bushes, draped over tree branches, or heaped in butcherlike piles of bone and viscera fused into unsightly lumps.

Claire trudged ahead, lips quivering, steps sinking into the quagmire of blood-soaked earth, wide eyes slowly taking in the entirety of the massacre she couldn't prevent. The stench was unbearable, but sharper still was the pain of failure—like a barbed chain ripping through her chest. The shattered leftovers of her comrades stared lifelessly into the void, their still eyes reflecting the pale glow of the moon. They were gone—all of them.

She stopped and tilted her face upward. Stars sparkled above, their tranquil brilliance indifferent to the carnage below. No green glow shimmered in the heavens, no trace of the hope she had chased so desperately.

Claire's heart clenched as the gruesome truth pressed down on her, crushing her chest. She had been right. It was too late.

***

A spark of electricity hissed through Gertrude's body, jolting her awake. It was similar to the one she'd felt from Claire. But this time, the intensity was tenfold.

Gertrude sat up, seething with anxiety.

Her spell was meant to alert her of the presence of anything bearing the touch of those creatures—like a prophetic alarm—and her powers had never failed before.

She remembered those first days of Company rule when witches and wizards were being executed in large numbers. She knew then she had to hide her magic to survive. Suppressing it had backfired for many, killing them painfully, or worse, turning them into something unspeakable. Gertrude had been keen to figure out another way, practicing her craft in the solitude of the woods at night, exploring, figuring out, learning the hard way. One morning, a woodcutter discovered her lying under a tree in a puddle of blood after a vein had ruptured in her ear.

It left her weak, but alive, and three days later, she was back in the woods to resume her research.

Months later, following many agonizing nights, she finally acquired the knowledge she sought. The key was to embrace it—to let the magic flow. Not as a vibrant brook in the open, but as a silent undercurrent beneath the veneer of an ordinary human. The balance was tricky, but with time, it became a habit.

Gertrude remembered it all, because the thought of *this* very night was what had kept her going all those years ago. She had to live back then, because she had to live *this* moment now.

The old woman gazed at the thin strands of blue lights sizzling down her palm. The omen was unmistakable.

Her hut was situated at a place which, from the eastern part of the woods, was the first point of entry to the nearest town. Gertrude had sinned in the past and this was her redemption—becoming the first one those creatures would cross paths with.

She closed her eyes and sucked in a slow, deep breath.

In the past, she had visualized this moment often, wondering how afraid she would be: every noise in the night had startled her; every sudden sound of a wing flutter had caused her heart to pound.

Gertrude opened her eyes, knowing the time had come.

To her surprise, she was not afraid.

CHAPTER 20

The landscape fringing the town of Lockewall sloped across the undulating terrain before rising up to the mountains in the distance. Tall grass carpeted the ground and dense trees soared up to the skies forming an almost impenetrable canopy.

Keith tiptoed through the trees, arrow drawn taut against his bowstring.

He was starving, and if he failed in his hunt, this would be his third straight day without food. Getting something worthy of a dinner was becoming increasingly difficult inside the town. And the mountain woods weren't safe at night. So, this middle ground was his favored hunting spot.

The place abounded with rabbits. With some perseverance, he could even strike a boar or a deer. Keith wouldn't have to worry about food for a week if he could get one of those. He forced the overly optimistic thoughts away to avoid getting distracted.

A faint sound. Keith straightened up, focused. Stepping behind a tree, he listened with his hunter's ears.

Flapping of wings!

He kept listening.

Enormous wings!

Keith crept through the dense foliage, his measured footfalls carrying the practiced grace of a skilled hunter. As he edged forward, the sound—a low, rhythmic flapping— grew louder, more insistent.

At the fringe of the gravelly path, he parted the last tangle of thicket. There, under the pale moonlight, stood the gnarled oak tree, its twisted branches clawing dark strands into the silver sky. Outlined against the moon hovered five massive shapes, their wings beating in perfect rhythm.

Keith's stomach rumbled with anticipation, but the hunger crumbled quickly into dread. With eyes burning like embers and feathers black as tar, the creatures were no ordinary birds. They were farther from anything Keith had ever imagined. His throat went dry, and a chill wound its way down his spine. Even the air around the creatures seemed to throb with something dark and sinister.

Then his heart lurched as something else drew his attention. On the ground near the cottage, a frail figure hunched in ritualistic motion, thin arms rising and falling with the vitality of a veteran conjurer. Bony fingers carved radiant, eerie lines through the air, each stroke illuminating her familiar visage. Keith watched with horror as Gertrude's lips moved rapidly in a soundless chant, her wrinkled face pulsing with a wild, fevered glow.

"The witch…" Keith's faint murmur drowned in the thumping in his chest. "Summoning her demons…"

He pressed himself lower to the ground, torn between a ghastly fascination with the horror unfolding before him and the primal urge to flee.

***

The dragons loomed over the oak tree—threshing, writhing, fighting to break the invisible restraints that chained them. Their screeches tore through the night, every beat of their jagged black wings a macabre emblem of the destruction they could unleash. Feet rooted to the ground, Gertrude chanted, tendrils of lights and shadows swirling around her fingers in an eerie, otherworldly display. Her withered body rocked to the rhythm of her mumbling, her powers locked in a silent but vicious battle against the darkness of ancient forces. The air crackled with the raw energies of spells forged through years of solitude and pain.

The words of spell flowed out of her like desperate prayers, meant at all costs to defeat the abominations she had spent her life preparing to face. This was her moment—to fulfil her purpose, to do her penance, to atone for a sin she had never fully comprehended yet felt in every aching bone: the sin of not seeing the loneliness in his eyes, of failing to love him enough until it was too late—until he had sought elsewhere, to the heavens, the love she could not give him. Her beloved Basil.

As Gertrude chanted, Basil's face emerged in front of her—young and handsome—the only man she had ever loved, the only soul that had ever touched her heart. She could almost feel his presence around. Hear his soft voice in her ears—his whispers of

103

promises that would never be fulfilled. If only she had loved him more. Just a little more.

Gertrude's chant faltered, but she steadied herself. Tonight, she would protect the place—the town she had once called home—from the creatures that had snatched Basil away from her. And in doing so, she might find the semblance of redemption she had been seeking for the past fifty years.

Out of nowhere, a sharp spasm of pain shot through her back. The chanting stopped. Her gaze went down to the pointed tip of an arrow, slick with blood, sticking out of her stomach.

The spell faltered, and the creatures' grumbling swelled. They thrashed harder against their invisible restraints.

Grabbing the head of the arrow, Gertrude pulled the shaft out. She opened her mouth to resume the chant, but another arrow hit her, perforating her lung.

She dropped to her knees, her blood-smeared hands trembling skyward in a frantic attempt to salvage the spell. Her mouth opened to chant, but the blood gurgled in her throat, choking the words. She watched helplessly as the dragons screeched and thrashed, their wings snapping as they shook off the daze—one by one.

Gertrude felt the gush of warm jets streaming up her throat, her breath dwindling away. For decades she had preserved herself for this inevitable face-off. Many thoughts had crossed her mind about how it would end; none as disappointing as this reality.

She turned her head.

Her assailant stood on the path a short distance away, armed with a bow and arrows.

Strength fading, Gertrude began to mutter her chant again. This time for a different spell.

*****

Keith gawped at the enormous birds charging down at him, but what alarmed him more was the witch's right hand ascending, her eyes pinned on him, as if she were about to direct her fury at him.

His finger flicked the bowstring again, sending a third arrow at her.

The shaft went through the center of her chest. Her body crumpled forward, limp, but a bolt had already left her hand.

The dragons bellowed, tearing free, their enormous wings thrashing like thunderclaps. The next moment, blazing torrents poured from the heavens—trails of fire converging on the old woman's fallen figure and erupting into a blinding inferno. The scorching tempest swelled outward in a fiery blast wave, devouring everything in its path.

Everything but the witch's bolt.

It shot from the raging flames—a relentless trident made of fierce, unyielding light, brighter than the conflagration itself—and wrapped around Keith just as the searing heat bore down, sealing him in a protective cocoon at the heart of the destruction.

CHAPTER 21

I want to see the commander-in-chief right now."

The head guard frowned at Claire and then at the two junior guards behind her.

"We tried to stop her," one of them explained.

"You can't just barge into this part of the castle, soldier," the head guard reprimanded her.

"*Right now,* I said." Claire made the urgency evident in her voice.

"It's past the commander-in-chief's bedtime."

"Then wake him up."

"Are you out of your mind?"

Claire decided to use the ace card up her sleeve. "Tell him I want to talk to him about Basil."

"Who?"

"Trust me, you don't want to know. Just tell him."

The head guard regarded her for a moment. "Wait here." He disappeared inside.

A minute later, he returned. "You can come in. He will see you."

Claire walked into the chamber, darkened except for the comforting flame in the hearth. Herbert lay in bed, his upper body propped on one elbow.

"You knew!" Claire hissed.

"Leave us," Herbert ordered.

The guard exited with a bow.

Herbert got up from the bed. "Come with me"

"Why did you do it?" Claire stood glaring at him.

"Not here." Herbert stepped into a narrow passageway. "Come."

Claire exhaled in frustration and followed him.

The end of the passage led them onto a balcony. He leaned on the railing as he spoke. "We all have our secrets," he said slowly. "Things we love and intend to protect."

"Even if it costs the lives of many?" Claire seethed.

"What do you mean?"

"They are dead. *All of them.*" Claire was fuming, "But for someone who knows what powers *actually* walk those woods, it never was a surprise, was it?"

"Watch yourself, soldier," Herbert snarled. "Don't forget who you are talking to."

"How can I?" Claire sneered with disdain.

He eyed her coldly. "We are done here."

"We all are, Commander." She turned to leave. "You allowed our soldiers to walk into the woods and hand those dragons the only thing they needed to break free of their cage."

Claire strode from the balcony, leaving behind a speechless Herbert, and found Rosaline standing in the dark of the passageway. Claire could tell the commander-in-chief's daughter had overheard their conversation.

She walked quickly from the chamber, rueful that she had inadvertently broken the news of Arthur's death to his wife.

CHAPTER 22

Nathan remained behind a pillar, watching as Claire crossed the courtyard toward the gatehouse. His hand went to the small knife hidden in the folds of his coat.

A touch of the blade to Claire's neck and Dawn would give herself to him out of gratitude. He would get to enjoy Lance's young widow. Nathan felt a tingle in his pants as he quietly picked up Claire's trail on the path outside the castle.

CHAPTER 23

"Artie suspected there were demons in the woods," Rosaline wailed. "And yet, instead of stopping him, you chose to let him die?"

The old man did not reply.

"Why, Father?"

The balcony overlooked the trees at the back of the castle. Herbert stood, his back turned to his daughter, his eyes on the waving silhouettes of birch below.

"*Why?*" she cried.

"Because," Herbert said slowly, "I had to."

Rosaline waited, but Herbert had nothing more to say.

She felt as if her insides had hollowed out. She couldn't tell what was more unbearable—knowing her husband was gone, or watching her father stand behind three inconceivable words of justification for widowing his only daughter. Her world belonged to two men, and suddenly both had ceased to exist.

"I hope it was worth it," Rosaline spat, her agony driving her to the only escape she could think of.

"Nooo!" Herbert lunged to grab her arm, but Rosaline had already leapt. He could only watch helplessly as his daughter plummeted toward the birch forest.

The dead stillness lasted only seconds before ending in a heavy thud hundreds of feet below.

CHAPTER 24

Flames danced over the debris. The air tasted of soot and burnt flesh, and the stench of destruction wafted through the dust. Lockewall had been turned into a burning sea of ruins, scattered with the gory leftovers of a savage feast.

Those who had tried to hide were incinerated under their shelters. Those who took a stand had been tortured and killed. Those who had sought to run from the horror were roasted alive.

Having reduced the city to bits, the demons glided across the red sky, locating whimpers in the rubble and swooping down to plough out their quarry from under the fallen roofs.

With every mouthful, their appetite mounted. And the more human souls they devoured, the bigger and stronger they grew.

Ophelia sat perched upon the smoldering carcass of a watchtower, gazing at Lockewall's wreck. She turned her attention to the northern horizon.

Next stop, *Winsden*.

CHAPTER 25

In the eastern part of the woods where the dark power had been at its strongest for all these years, the grounds retained no footprints. As the land sloped away from that area, the magic slowly waned, and beyond the drooping branches of the big willow tree downhill, the enchantment was fully absent.

Signs of activity could be seen beneath the willow—trampled bushes, dislocated chunks of rocks, and other signatures left behind by the soldiers earlier in the night.

All the boot marks moved up the hill from the tree, but only one set came down. They belonged to a soldier who had abandoned his men and ran for his life—*a deserter*.

CHAPTER 26

Herbert leaned against the balustrade, unmoving, hand outstretched, his mind frantically replaying the most painful moment of his life again and again. Each time, in a relentless loop, he managed to catch his daughter. He held her close, made amends for the pain he had caused, eased her anguish with acts that existed only in a father's desperate, alternate reality.

The old man's mind roiled until all that remained was a gaping void—an emptiness widening inside, swallowing everything. He pulled away from the railing and slumped to the balcony floor, surrendering to the punishment of reality. His beautiful daughter—the only thing he had ever truly loved—was gone.

Slowly, Herbert forced himself to his feet. There was nothing to hold him back now. He turned to the birch forest, blasts of strong wind pounding his face.

Climbing the balustrade, he tucked his heels into the narrow sill and gripped the rails behind him. It was the only way to end this once and for all. He looked down. The treetops below swayed gently—reminders of the wrongs he couldn't right.

Herbert let go, plunging into the darkness.

But there was no thud.

Just before Herbert's plummeting form hit the ground, it transformed into a small, but majestic, black dragon which soared up to the sky, blazing away into the night.

CHAPTER 27

Everything happened so suddenly."

"We tried to rescue her."

"By the time I broke in through the window, it was too late."

The words from the crowd flew past Claire, failing to register in her mind. They didn't matter. Nothing mattered anymore. She remained wilted on her knees, eyes fixed on Alice lying still like the blackened trunk of a dead tree.

From the back of a hut, Nathan observed Claire. The village was overflowing with people, but they were distracted. And something told Nathan that the moment had come. He blended into the crowd.

Ringlets of smoke rose to the sky from the wreck of burnt logs—the last breaths of the place Claire had called home for years. She stared at the heartbreaking reminder of the memories she had made in there with the only person to have ever cared for her—her darling Alice.

Nathan edged through the crowd, reaching within ten yards of his target. One quick stab into her back while brushing past her, and it would be over. By the time they noticed it, he'd be gone—on his way to present the blood-drenched knife to Dawn and claim his prize. It was all laid out so perfectly in his head.

Claire's face twitched. She'd heard someone say, "I saw a man torch the place with my own two eyes." Forcing herself to her feet, she turned her head in search for the speaker—and that's when she saw him. She knew the look in his eyes, but paralyzed by grief, she did not react.

Nathan paused, startled. He wavered for a moment but decided it was too late to turn back. Quietly yanking the blade out of his pocket, he charged at her, unaware his hasty act had put him in the line of fire of Claire's other enemy lurking in the crowd, their sights set on the same woman.

Seconds before the blade touched Claire, a gunshot rang out. The knife clattered to the ground and Nathan collapsed beside it, dead.

Shocked silence engulfed the crowd instantly. Then someone pointed at a man furtively sneaking away.

"That's him! He killed Alice."

CHAPTER 28

Aurelia, Winter, Noah, River, and Ophelia raced through the skies. Drifting clouds blocked their view, but they didn't need to see. The richly populated town was close by, and the depraved angels could tell.

As they neared the outskirts of Winsden, Ophelia slowed down. Her superior senses had picked up something the others had not.

The four of them disappeared in the cloudy sky ahead, just as a silhouette rocketed at Ophelia from below.

It cannoned into her, knocking her away. Ophelia swerved and charged back, but the tiny black dragon ducked under the blow, striking her again using a deft combat technique.

Unhurt, Ophelia turned, slashing her claw like a thunderbolt, but the little dragon dodged it with a skillful glide, vanishing into the clouds.

In the next moment, she felt a knock on her back and then to her side.

The enormous dragon stared into the clouds, tricked by the strategy of hide-and-strike. Her undersized adversary was utilizing its agility against her. Ophelia smirked, invigorated by the challenge. But she had no desire to prolong it.

The clouds were her enemy's ally. She inhaled deeply, and then exhaled a stream of hot air.

CHAPTER 29

Claire watched as the men pinned down the assassin, holding his left arm firmly outstretched.

A big, swarthy fellow heaved a rock over his head and smashed it on the man's hand.

He gave out a cry as his fingers imploded with a crunch.

"It will be the other hand next," declared the swarthy man. "Who sent you?"

The assassin gritted his teeth in pain. "The commander-in-chief!"

A tremor of shock rattled Claire. She stood in astounded silence, unable to believe her ears.

But just then, flaming beams rained down, striking people nearby.

"Demons!"

"Run!"

Everyone gawped at the sky, scampering in terror.

The onslaught intensified, driving down on the rows of houses, flooding into the streets, and drowning the screams of alarm in hot, yellow torrents.

A shed burst into flames, hurling Claire into the air, and smashing her into a wall, scrambling the thoughts in her head—rearranging snippets of Gertrude's words with things Herbert had told her.

And suddenly, it all made sense to her.

Everything.

CHAPTER 30

Ophelia's scalding breath burned away the clouds. The smaller dragon lunged, but before it could strike, she caught it in her claws.

"Get out of my town, you monster!" it roared.

"Naïve, little Herbert…" Ophelia's twisted mouth curled into a sinister grin. "Blinded, beaten and thrown into the woods in his friend's clothes—the boy never really understood why he was sent to become the first victim of the curse."

The dragon writhed, but her grip only tightened as her powers tore through his mind.

"So many executed in the name of witch-killing—because you feared they might expose your own dark secret. A secret you buried under a stolen name. The moment anyone whispered of dark magic in the woods, you silenced them—whether a lowly soldier or your own son-in-law."

Her voice dripped with mockery. "And yet, you call *me* the monster?"

She traced the lightning scar on his neck with a razor-sharp nail. "The cage that held us in the eastern woods never bound you, because you were a human. But you never truly were, were you? You've always been ten times the monster I could ever be—Basil."

"I was protecting my daughter," he cried.

"Yes—that's what you told yourself," Ophelia hissed, driving her claw deeper into his skull. "You hid the history of magic in her blood, hoping no one—not even the Company—would see her as a threat. But if you truly loved her more than your own skin…" Her grin widened. "…why did you kill her?"

Basil's eyes narrowed in fury. He wrenched back his folded wing and thrust it at her chest, but she caught it with ease and ripped it away. His scream shook the air. "Don't you see?" Ophelia scoffed. "Nothing in your mind is hidden from me."

And yet one truth slipped past her, hidden in plain sight.

Basil writhed, rage twisting into something else. When he finally spoke, his voice broke—not with fury, but with grief.

"Then you know," he wailed, "my heart has always belonged to you."

Ophelia's eyes blazed like magma, the eruption of a long-dormant volcano. She raised her twisted, reptilian limb above her head and roared, "And look what it made of me!"

With the savage fury of the beast she had become, Ophelia tore into her lover's chest, sinking her fangs into his beating black heart. Her jaws crushed it to pulp before she ripped it free of his lifeless body.

Moments later, the walls of Winsden trembled with Ophelia's earth-shattering roar. It was filled with fury and hate, but beneath it all, those who heard could sense the sorrow of love lost.

CHAPTER 31

Claire woke up, coughing out dirt. The right side of her face felt sticky, her head throbbing. She wiped the haze from her eyes and peered through the rolling waves of dust. She was lying against the broken wall of a shed, unable to recall what had hit her. The street was filled with mangled, charred corpses, scattered among burning chunks of debris. The hot sky glowed through dusty clouds—giant, flying silhouettes streaking against the crimson. One of them glided down and roosted over a chimney across the street.

Claire gasped. The creature seemed to have grown at least four times bigger.

An infant was weeping over a woman's body nearby.

Claire observed the dragon. It was digging something from the debris. She crawled to the baby quietly.

The dragon yanked out a man. Wounded and bleeding, he pleaded for his life.

Picking the baby girl up, Claire shuffled to a hut as fast as she could.

The beast crunched the man's head, ripped it off from his shoulders, and then turned its gaze down the path.

In the next moment, the place lit up with a blinding dash of light. Claire squealed out as a flaming whip lashed on her from behind. She shielded the baby in her arms, her back sizzling in fire.

The dragon flew to her and perched on an adjacent roof as she wriggled on the ground, screaming, rubbing her back in the dirt to douse the flames on her clothes.

The beast just quietly watched her.

Putting out the fire, she shoved the baby behind the hut and crawled back to the center of the street.

"Why are you destroying everything?" she shouted, her teeth gnashing to fight the pain.

The creature studied her silently.

"You used to help humans, love humans, remember? And they'd love you back. What changed?" Claire dragged herself down the street, drawing the beast's focus with her. "Oh wait, I guess no one can love a face *that* ugly, right, fucker?"

The reptile's eyes narrowed. It snorted, the hairs on its neck standing up.

"So, why not be a big fat bitch and grab some attention, huh?"

The dragon inhaled a long, menacing breath, and Claire could tell it was filling its chest with enough to set the entire place ablaze. She edged as far as she could from the baby, preparing herself for what was coming.

Just as the dragon opened its mouth to empty its lungs, a blazing globe rocketed through the air and shot inside its mouth. The creature tried to spit it out, but the burning ball seemed to have lodged itself in its gullet immovably.

The dragon leaped into the air, its wings flailing, and spiraled upward in a crooked, out-of-control ascent as luminous cracks split wider across its body. Then the volatile breath within its chest exploded, and the enormous creature burst apart, lighting up the skies in a spectacular firework.

CHAPTER 32

Two dragons circled above the place where their companion had fallen. Arthur had no time to waste. He dashed into the arsenal and checked the trough—barely enough pig fat remained for one more shot. The rest of the arsenal was empty; this was the last of the inflammable paste. A quick glance outside confirmed his fear: the creatures were moments from realizing what had struck one of their brethren. Smearing the projectile with the remaining fat, he raced back to the ballista.

But one of the dragons had already caught the attacker's scent.

Arthur looked from the approaching silhouette to the ballista. He would never manage to load it in time. And even if he did, a flaming shot would be useless against a dragon already on guard.

Arthur snatched up his rifle and turned south. The watchtower stood twenty yards away. The creature rocketed toward him as he scrambled over the rocks. His rifle was empty; the slugs clanked uselessly in his pocket, and there was no time to load. The screeching hammered into his ears, louder every instant, and Arthur knew only a miracle could get him through the tower door alive.

As the dragon unleashed its fury, an arrow shot from a nearby roof, glanced off its wing, and spun away. The strike jarred the beast just enough—the torrent of fire slammed into the rocks, yards short of its mark, exploding into a flaming gust that knocked Arthur off his feet. He crashed through the tower door, hitting the floor hard. Pain shot up his arm, but he barely noticed. He fumbled for the slugs in his pocket just as the door splintered apart and the enormous beast stormed in through the debris.

Arthur clambered to his feet.

The dragon paused, trying to locate him through the dust, then lunged at Arthur as he shuffled up the staircase that coiled around the wall to the roof. Arthur ducked away from the sweeping blow which wiped out the lower set of steps. Arthur leaped off and climbed up to higher ground. The beast struck again, and this time, a searing pain shot up his body. The slugs slipped from his grip and clattered away. He grabbed the wall, groaning, hobbling up, knowing there was no turning back. The steps behind him blasted into pieces as the dragon kept hacking and pounding blindly at its target through the thick cloud of flying debris.

The wall at the side ended, and Arthur found himself on the roof. He fumbled in his pockets—one slug left.

The dragon raged onto the roof, glowering at the tiny figure pointing a rifle at it.

Arthur was aware they were immune to bullets, but he had also seen enough back in the woods to know a shot through the heart disabled them for a while.

The creature sat back on its haunches, as if it were toying with its quarry before tearing it apart.

Arthur aimed at the center of its chest and squeezed the trigger. A stiff clack, and then the weapon jammed. The dragon stepped closer. Arthur backed away, his finger desperately tugging at the lever. The beast raised its claws.

Arthur shot a glance behind him—he was at the edge of the roof.

Instead of tearing him apart, the dragon gently tapped on his chest and pushed him over. As Arthur fell, he drove the rifle upward, the bayonet piercing its heart and wrenching a weak wail from the beast.

Clinging to the rifle's butt, his legs flailed over the edge, scraping for footholds on the wall.

The creature clawed the blade, trying to wrench it free, but failed. Its drooping gaze lifted skyward as it loosed a ragged cry, flames sputtering in pale yellow and red before its body crumbled into ash.

Arthur plummeted, his mind a blur of confusion. Yet just before the rocks rushed up to meet him, his final thoughts were not of fear or pain. They were of redemption for deserting his men in the woods.

They were of peace.

CHAPTER 33

S*trike the heart!"*
  "Shoot them down!"
  "Burn them!"

The noises below weren't just roars of anger. They had something more powerful in them. Hope!

Ophelia's scaled wings cast their shadow over the half-destroyed town as she soared across a sky stained scarlet by fire. She gazed at the wreckage she had wrought, a flicker of contentment in her chest. Yet something else stirred within her—a voice she thought she had buried long ago. It told her to stop. But Ophelia raged on.

Enormous sabers of flames poured from her jaws, ripping through the debris and illuminating the tiny silhouettes of archers crouched in the alleys, bowstrings taut, eyes locked on the embodiment of annihilation sweeping over their rooftops.

The voice tugged at her like a ghostly whisper—weak, haunting, reminding her of the self she had once been.

Below her, houses burned. The dead lay in the streets. The living either cowered in fear or sought her end.

Ophelia's heart throbbed with a strange heaviness, wringing itself with every beat. Her face twitched—hesitation, or even softness, flickering in her gaze. She shut her eyes and soared higher, the wind brushing her scales like a memory of another life: when she had been beautiful, when she had been an angel, when she had fallen in love.

With Basil.

She opened her eyes. The softness was gone. She brought herself to a halt mid-sky. An arrow sliced up at her from one of the alleys. Ophelia stared down. Flames licked through the ruins, mingling with screams of people and twangs of bowstrings. The frail voice mumbled inside her again, pleading this time, echoing with memories of who she truly was. But Ophelia let anger consume her. She clenched her jaw—snuffing out the faint whisper under a flood of vengeance—and barreled towards the ground, unleashing her wrath into the alleys. Her flaming breath erupted in an unending torrent, bursting through doors, smashing walls to smithereens, streaming into every crack and corner. Houses exploded, screams multiplied, and bodies wrapped in flames thudded on the ground. She blazed across, drowning the archers in a ruthless wave of conflagration.

When the arrows finally stopped coming, Ophelia's fury slowly relented. She descended, alighting over a shattered roof. Corpses littered the rubble around her. She glanced down at the arrow butts sticking out of her scaled hide and sneered. However, something felt… wrong. Her gaze surveyed the sky, looking for her companions. But her vision swam, a weird discomfort crawling under her scales.

As she staggered a little, memories flashed before her. She saw herself, not as this hideous creature, but as the embodiment of divinity—the one long-lost and forgotten—brimming with kindness and warmth. Her eyes welled up at the thought of the curse that had tainted her all those years ago, turned her light into shadows, morphing her divinity into this demonic vessel of rage, retribution, and endless hunger. The voice inside her was no longer a whisper. It was a cry of loss—a wail reminding her of everything she had once been.

Ophelia wrenched an arrow from her flesh, her claws trembling. She tried to roar, but all that escaped her was a gasp—ragged and shallow. Strength dwindling, her body stumbled under the weight of wounds which, only moments ago, would have meant nothing.

Holding out her claw, she eyed it. Pieces from it were scattering like embers in the wind. Ophelia collapsed on the floor, feeling herself slipping away, and in those final moments, she saw it all—the choices she had made, the illusion of invincibility that had clouded her judgment, the connection that bound her to the others—she figured with piercing clarity every single thing that had brought her to this end.

A tear rolled down her scaled cheek as her huge form slowly dissolved into countless motes of luminous dust, just a single question lingering in her: Was she really wrong?

142

CHAPTER 34

Metallic weapons clanked in the hands of the mob thumping over the scourged landscape, searching.

"Eyes up!" Claire hollered, firearm pointed above, the baby strapped to her chest in a cloth sling.

The sky was a dusty curtain of black and undulating red.

"Can't see them no more!" a boy remarked.

Gazes raked through the swirling fumes of ash and dust, but the flying reptiles could not be seen anymore.

"They are gone!" cried a woman.

"We have scared them away." Someone gave a jubilant roar.

Claire peered around. The dragons seemed to have vanished. The creatures she had thought indestructible had been slain—at least three of them, and she had no idea how.

She didn't care. All that mattered was that the remaining two were gone.

Suddenly, a swooping whoosh came from behind. Before she could turn, sickles cut into the fresh burn on her back, lifting her off the ground, and she howled in pain.

"It's taking her." A boy pointed to the sky.

"Shoot it."

The dragon rose higher as a stray arrow ran through her thigh, but Claire sensed nothing—she had already passed out.

"Stop!" a woman on the ground barked at the archers. "There's nothing we can do."

They stood in silence, watching the dragon—and Claire—disappear through the layers of smoke.

***

Claire awoke, splinters of excruciating pain shooting through her wounds. She looked up, her vision a sea of hazy, black dots swimming in a dizzying rhythm, but she could make out the hulking shadow flapping its wings over her.

The baby!

Claire's hands leaped to her chest. The baby lay motionless, tucked against her body.

A fiery gust grazed past her, lighting the fog of black dots up in a blinding flood. Cannons thundered below. Guns rang out. Screams of people dwarfed the explosions.

Bullets whistled past her.

She lifted her head slightly, and a white-hot agony ripped through her flesh, as a stray bullet found its unintended target in her arm.

Then silence. As suddenly as the cacophony had begun.

Claire sensed hard ground beneath her, and she leaned back. The impact was soft, yet, it felt like burning hammer blows on her wounded body.

Ash particles floating in the air carried the familiar stench of destruction.

Claire glanced around, wisps of blood-drenched hair streaking her face.

Corpses lined the parapet walk, some still on fire. An overturned cannon gaped at her from some distance away, and the floor lay scattered with metal shields and smoking footwear. Claire realized she was sitting atop the castle's battlements—one of the highest points in Winsden.

A snouted face hung over her, its right canine missing.

And then it all came back to her.

Her shaking hands reached for the baby, but a long, sharp claw traced across her chest, slicing through the cloth that bound the infant to her. The unmoving child slipped beyond reach. Claire looked at the dragon. Hunger burned in its eyes—but behind it, she thought she glimpsed something else: a wounded pride, an insult never forgotten.

The creature's face drew closer, its breath stinging her skin—slow, deliberate.

Claire winced. The horrors from two nights ago flooded back as the low rumble reverberated down her neck. She had escaped this creature once; now it was time to pay.

"You know what?" Claire forced out, her voice shaking. "Come back after you've showered—I'll wait." She dragged herself back in mock disgust, praying he couldn't see the terror in her eyes.

The dragon's eye twitched. It straightened, spread its wings, and leapt into the air.

Claire watched, wide-eyed, as the enormous reptile soared upward, then circled back, its body shifting midair into that of a majestic angel. A radiant halo crowned him, shedding light across the devastation as he descended once more.

"Last time we met, you had missed this sight," he said, his voice a dulcet melody, "and the fun. Try not to swoon this time."

Claire gaped at his divine form, then caught herself. "I'm glad I did."

"Why's that?"

"Coz you're an agony to the eye."

The stunningly handsome face hardened, and he bent over her.

She tried to draw back, but he pinned her to the ground, his gaze locked on hers. "I'll show you what agony is," he hissed.

Claire watched as the angel's hand slid up her leg to her thigh. She braced herself, staring into that serene, unyielding face.

The angel seized the shaft protruding above her knee—and twisted.

Claire gritted her teeth.

"Does it hurt?" He twisted it harder.

Claire pounded the asphalt with her fist but choked back the screams.

"No?" He bent the shaft sideways and tore it from her leg. "How about now?"

Claire's lungs exploded in a cry. She writhed, blood soaking her pants.

The angel turned to the hole in her arm. He stroked the bullet wound almost tenderly—then drove his finger into it. Claire squealed.

He watched her thrash on the ground and smiled.

Claire dragged herself back, tears streaking through the blood on her face. "Is that all you got?" she wheezed.

The angel's smile vanished. He started to speak, but a distant screech echoed across the sky. He turned west. Over the smoking rows of houses, a dragon plunged from the heavens, its body riddled with shafts and lances. Growling, wings flailing, it disintegrated to dust before it hit the ground.

"Last man standing, huh?" Claire chuckled.

The angel glared at her, then snarled. "Enough!"

Claire saw him suck in a deep breath. Summoning the last of her strength, she hauled herself toward a discarded metal shield and pulled it close just as the angel spat fires. She hunched under the plate as a burst of flames slammed into it—short, but searing.

"Below average!" She flung aside the red-hot chunk of metal and kept dragging herself back. "Guess you'll have to turn into that less-ugly thing to do better."

His eyes narrowed. He shoed the shield away like a dried leaf and drew in another breath.

Claire looked around.

There was nothing left to shield her this time.

Noah filled his lungs, but something felt wrong inside him. His strength—his very life force—had withered, as though aged by thousands of years.

"Looks like you're out of firepower, dickhead," Claire mocked.

It should have been a moment of contemplation— a chance for Noah to face the truth of his lost power and immortality. But blinded by arrogance, he let fury consume him. He lunged at Claire, seizing her by the neck.

She tried to speak, but the words died in her throat as Noah's grip crushed her windpipe.

"Not so chatty now, are you?" he spat through clenched teeth.

Claire's arms and legs thrashed against the debris, raking through smoldering scraps, but found nothing useful.

Noah squeezed harder, cartilage crackling beneath his fingers. His other hand began to roam her body.

Claire's face flushed crimson beneath the streaks of blood, her eyes bulging. With the last of her fading strength, her thumb flicked a small burning fragment across the floor. It rolled away glowing faintly.

"I could have finished you with a single blow." Noah grinned, one hand choking her, the other hand stroking her like a lover. "But where is the fun in that?"

Claire's mouth hung open. Her fingers clawed at his iron grip—scratching, tugging—before falling limp at her sides.

Almost.

"I can't wait to see the look in those eyes when they—"

Noah stopped, flinching back. A faint sizzle hissed nearby, but he ignored it.

In that instant of distraction, Claire pulled herself back—wheezing, hawking, dragging in air like a drowning woman breaking the surface.

Noah sat speechless. His frown hardened, but his gaze dulled into stupor as his mind wrestled with the impossible. He hadn't looked inward—into the core of his power, bound to the other angels by a single spirit. If he had, he might have realized the truth: devouring Basil's heart had tainted Ophelia's very essence, and through her, the rest of them. He might have seen that Basil, after suppressing his dark magic for fifty years, had become something so vile—so wretchedly corrupt—that the plague in his heart was strong enough to corrode even the strongest and darkest of forces.

But Noah did not see. And in the haze that gripped him, nothing seemed to matter —not the dulling of his senses, not the strange stillness creeping into his strength, not even the fact that Claire, in her desperate struggle, had flicked one of the burning chunks of debris across the ground... sending it rolling into the cannon's exposed fuse.

The sizzle sharpened into a searing hiss. Claire rolled across the ground, slammed her heel against the cannon's rear, and wrenched the muzzle toward him—just as the barrel jolted with a thunderous burst.

"You—" Noah began, his slack-jawed gaze still fixed on the hand that had stroked Claire's belly.

An iron ball shot out of the muzzle.

"...are bearing my chil—"

***

Claire watched the angel hurtle off from the roof. His body slammed into the north tower, and the lead shrapnel packed into the iron ball burst apart, spraying the courtyard below with hundreds of glowing fragments of the angel's body.

Claire roared in triumph, laughing—arms flung wide as she lay on her back.

But then the remembered voices rose in her mind.

...the marks on the rest of your body are their lust...

A male angel is very likely to lust over certain female humans.

Last time we met, you missed this sight and the fun.

Her hysterical laughter cracked, broke, and became an anguished scream. The words merged, jumbled, swelled— filling the void of her memory with hideous, half-formed images of what might have happened before she'd woken to Tim's gunshot that night in the woods.

And how do the rules apply to those hideous shape-shifters?

I don't know. Nobody does. And you should pray it stays that way.

Gertrude's horrified face flashed before her eyes.

Claire's cries ebbed to a long, heart-wrung howl.

You are bearing my chil—

The angel's unfinished words rang in her skull like an ominous knell. She gritted her teeth, willing every last trace of him from her mind. Other thoughts gushed in—dark, crushing thoughts.

Alice was gone, so were hundreds of others—men and women she had grown up with, officers she'd served under, soldiers she had fought beside. The idea of them dead carved out a terrible emptiness that made Alice's absence ache even more.

She rolled to her side, spent and trembling. Her eyes settled on the tiny bundle of cloth near the parapet—still, unmoving. Her heart sank, a deep sadness wrapping her like a shroud.

That helpless little creature was the last thing she had tried to protect.

And she'd failed her too.

What good is this life anymore?

A cold shiver crept under her blood-soaked garments. Claire curled up into herself, drawing her knees to her chest, no longer resisting the soft, numbing drowsiness overtaking her.

She closed her eyes and let it pull her down into darkness—a darkness she would never wake from.

152

CHAPTER 35

The early morning stillness shattered with a sharp cry.

Forcing her eyes open, Claire peered over at the pile of cloth on the other side of the roof, certain the movement beneath it wasn't the tugging of the morning breeze.

The baby!

Claire dragged herself toward it, her drowsiness ebbing away.

154

EPILOGUE

As dawn broke, the sun cast a pale shimmer across the town of Winsden. Corpses lay scattered across layers of debris carpeting the land. Shards of broken steel gleamed in the rubble as smoke thinned into the morning sky.

Crowned by the first light of day, the castle on the hill gazed down at the receding remnants of night—slowly revealing the magnitude of the devastation below.

Behind its rear walls, the uninhabited woods stretched for more than a mile. There, little seemed to have changed. The treetops waved in the breeze; the hum of waking insects and the trills of birds began to reclaim the air.

A doe bounded between the trees. Butterflies rose around her in a golden dance—the birth of a beautiful new day.

As her path carried her through the woods, her hooves churning moss dark with blood, she passed a hunched shape beneath a tree.

She drifted into a gentle skip but froze, ears pricked, as though the air had whispered something into them. Her eye flickered; a tremor rippled through her body before her legs buckled and she collapsed to the ground.

The hunched shape stirred, rising to its feet—neck twisted, limbs mangled and warped. It loomed over the fallen doe, one hand outstretched, as if drawing something unseen from her body. The creature convulsed once, then went still.

The shadowy figure staggered away, bones snapping back into place with a grisly chorus of crackles.

At the edge of a tall thicket, the figure turned—daylight catching a face once beautiful, now hideously unrecognizable beneath a shroud of dark magic.

Rosaline.

VICTOR NANDI

VICTOR NANDI writes dark fantasy, crime, thriller, and sci-fi.

His works have featured in books from several publication houses around the world.

When he isn't working or writing, he is probably trying to cheer up a friend with a horror story, or boring his colleagues with sermons on diet, travel, workouts, and the incredible power of reading. Some of his shorter pieces can be found in Black Hare Press anthologies.

Bibliography

Cosmos, Ghost Orchid Press, 2021

Forest Of Fear, Blood Song Books, 2021

Gluttony, Black Hare Press, 2021

Lost Lore and Legend, Breaking Rules Publishing, 2021

Love Me, Love Me Not, Black Hare Press, 2023

Rogue Tales, Dragon Soul Press, 2022
Year Four, Black Hare Press, 2023

Connect
Facebook: @victor.nandi.92
LinkedIn: linkedin.com/in/victor-nandi-487aa3125
Instagram: @victor.nandi_

BLACK HARE PRESS

Black Hare Press is a small, independent publisher based in Melbourne, Australia.

Founded in 2018, our aim has always been to champion emerging authors from all around the globe and offer opportunities for them to participate in speculative fiction and horror short story anthologies.

Connect: linktr.ee/blackharepress

ACKNOWLEDGEMENTS

Every story begins with an idea, but it takes many hearts to bring it to life.

To Victor Nandi, for crafting this haunting world and trusting Black Hare Press to help bring it from the shadows.

To our Patreon supporters—S. Jade Path, Rob Voss, and James Aitchison—your ongoing support keeps the darkness alive and the words flowing. We're endlessly grateful for your belief in what we do.

To our incredible Read Team, whose sharp eyes and tireless dedication ensure every page meets the light in its best form—your commitment makes all the difference.

And to our readers—thank you for stepping into the gloom with us, for turning each page, and for keeping independent horror burning bright.

Love & kisses, The Team